NICK RAN AFTER HIS PARTNER, TAKING THE ESCALATOR STAIRS FIVE AT A CLIP . . .

He was in an underground parking garage, vast and dark and smelling of grease and danger.

Nick spotted Charlie about 50 yards away, edging carefully toward the black-helmeted biker.

With an ear-splitting howl, three more bikes appeared from different corridors of the vast underground maze. Charlie spun around as the bikers streaked past him from all directions. They taunted him, passing close enough to reach out and prick him with the steel that glinted in their hands.

They spun around, sticking it to him over and over, and then suddenly they sped away. Charlie, grabbing his stomach, staggered a step or two. Blood poured out from between his hands.

"Charlie!" Nick shouted, sprinting toward him.

He was too late. The biker got there first. He had thrown off his helmet, and even as he ran toward Charlie, Nick recognized Sato.

Charlie stumbled backward. Screeching a guttural yell, Sato charged in, holding up the gleaming blade of his *tanto*.

"Charlie!" Nick yelled. He had never felt so helpless in his life . . .

BLACK RAIN

A novel by Mike Cogan
from the screenplay written by
Craig Bolotin & Warren Lewis

POCKET BOOKS

New York   London   Toronto   Sydney   Tokyo

An *Original* Publication of POCKET BOOKS

POCKET BOOKS, a division of Simon & Schuster Inc.
1230 Avenue of the Americas, New York, NY 10020

This book is published by Pocket Books,
a division of Simon & Schuster Inc.,
under exclusive license from Paramount
Pictures Corporation.

ISBN: 0-671-68969-X

First Pocket Books printing September 1989

10 9 8 7 6 5 4 3 2 1

POCKET and colophon are trademarks of
Simon & Schuster Inc.

Printed in the U.S.A.

BLACK RAIN

1

*B*righton Beach is the place, after Coney Island, where Brooklyn meets the Atlantic Ocean in an abrupt confrontation. Avenues dead-end at the board-walk. There is a long boulevard following the curve of the shoreline where traffic plays dodge'em around the pillars of the elevated train. On the beach, waves crash onto the broad expanse of sand between wooden pavilions built nearly a hundred years ago. Along the boulevard there are shops and restaurants, blini bak-eries and Muscovian nightclubs, because this is the Russian emigré colony—but on Sundays, especially in the wintertime, the shops are closed and traffic slows almost to a stop.

At one of the intersections where avenues meet the boardwalk, it is the habit of bikers to congregate on out-of-season Sundays. The roaring and revving of their motors vie with the screech of the overhead trains and the rhythmic pounding of the surf.

One grungy food stand, not classy enough to qualify as a joint, maintains a tenuous hold on a little ramp that leads from the sidewalk up to the boardwalk. It's no more than a lean-to and seems to sway in the icy winter wind coming across the beach from the sea. Summer and winter, year after year, the owner serves up Puerto Rican meat pies, kosher hot dogs, and vile but piping-hot coffee.

Nick Conklin, a squarely built, rugged fellow you might think was a bit too old for the motorcycle scene, set his helmet down on the counter and nodded hi to the owner, who handed him a cup of steaming coffee. Nick took off his gloves and shoved them into the pockets of his leather jacket. Then he warmed his hands around the Styrofoam.

As he sipped his coffee he watched the action at the intersection. There might have been thirty or more bikers—all kinds, from street rats and hard cases to gentlemanly tourists whose bikes were equipped with saddlebags and wives. Several wire trash baskets had been set afire and the riders congregated around them, keeping warm and swapping bullshit. These biker types tended to segregate themselves in a sort of natural selection. Nick's attention was on a newcomer, who was young and pony-tailed, wearing leather made heavy with studs, showing off a slick new Japanese factory bike.

"Give me one of them meat pies," came a voice at his elbow. Nick turned and grinned.

"Hi, Frankie."

"Yo, Nick," the man said. He was a slack-eyed

grifter with skin the color and consistency of mayonnaise. He was watching the new kid, too.

"What do you think?" Nick asked. Frankie just shrugged and picked up the *pastito* from the paper plate in front of him. His eyes never left the action.

"What can you do me?" Nick asked.

Frankie bit into the meat pie. The red juice squirted down his chin and meandered through the stubble. "No particular limit," he said, chewing. The wind whipped his sparse hair.

Nick's eyes narrowed. He was a good-looking man in his early forties, with sandy-to-brown hair just grazing his shoulders, more from reluctance to get a haircut than any kind of fashion statement. He was in his Sunday best—jeans, boots, Navy surplus turtleneck sweater, and leather jacket. He squinted at the newcomer, bouncing on his shiny new seat, revving his engines like he just couldn't wait. "Why? You seen him run?"

"Don't have to," Frankie said. "He's young stuff and there ain't nothing in that helmet but hair."

Nick grinned. "Make it a hundred," he said.

Frankie put down his food and dug into his jacket pocket, coming up with a greasy hundred-dollar bill, a pencil stub, and a dog-eared notebook. He handed the bill to Nick and made an entry in the book.

"You ask me, you should find a better way to spend your Sundays," he said.

"Like what?"

Frankie stuffed the last of the greasy pie in his mouth and wiped his hands on the paper napkin that it had been wrapped in. "They run a good church up the street," he said seriously.

Nick laughed and shook his head. "Anybody on their knees in this town ain't praying," he said. With a gesture like thanks-and-see-you-later, he left the stand and saddled up on the modified Harley he'd parked at the end of the ramp. One push and it started humming. He wove his way slowly through the clusters of bikers, with a lot of hellos and how-ya-doin's.

He closed in on the street rats with their shiny Hondas and Suzukis. The kid was only about nineteen. He was leaning on his bright red bike. Nick nudged his wheels through the crowd and came up closer, looked over the bike while the kid sat proudly revving up as much noise as he had.

"Is it quick?" Nick asked.

The kid looked at Nick, looked at the Harley, and snorted. "Shit," he said. "The box it came in is quicker than that sled." He grinned at his own witticism and looked around for appreciation, but most of the others knew enough about Nick's reputation not to laugh at his bulky old customized bike.

"For how much?" Nick asked casually. The rising decibels of *varoooom varoooom* all around them signaled some of the excitement that was building. Bikes were circling around, coming in closer.

The kid looked at Nick for a minute, and then, unsmiling, pulled on his helmet. He bounced down on the gas and led Nick out of the crowd to the boulevard.

The best straightaway for racing was closer to the Coney Island section of the beachfront, and within minutes the bikers had a caravan going west to the site. Having declined all offers of a ride on someone's back, Frankie led the way in his beat-up, but wholly-owned, medallion cab. They roared onto Neptune

Avenue. Past the aquarium, the gutted remains of the amusement area loomed up like ghosts of summers past. Here, in the dead of winter, all was truly deserted except for the parade of bikers eager for action.

Frankie got out of his cab and determined where the starting line would be. Bets came down fast and furious. The bikers arranged themselves along the race path. Nick on his Harley and the kid astride his Japanese marvel lined up alongside Frankie.

"Take a side bet?" Nick asked the kid.

"I'll take your social security!" He thought he was funny.

"Fifty says you don't live to see the season," Nick told him.

"Hey, fuck y—"

The kid was cut off as Frankie raised a burning road flare over his head. He dropped his arm and both bikes left rubber as they accelerated down the block.

The kid had the guts and the turbocharge. Nick had the experience. The streets had some of New York's finest potholes. The two bikes came around the first turn dead-even. At the next curve, the kid leaned low, edging Nick toward the hard curb, trying to cut him off. Nick laid on the power and shot past before the kid could squeeze him. Impressed with Nick's finesse, the kid fell behind, but only for a split-second. He gunned it.

They were doing ninety on pitted roads that would be hazardous even at a safe speed. Nick was leading, opening it up for a short block before the next turn. Behind him, the kid poured on the power and came roaring up alongside. They made it neck-and-neck at the final curve.

Suddenly the kid spotted a treacherous pothole looming up in front of him like death. Swerving, he leaned into Nick, sending him into a spin.

A less skilled rider, or maybe just a less lucky one, would have spun out and over. There was no way to avoid it—but Nick managed to stay on the bike when it was down, and then he righted it fast and went after the kid with everything he had.

Skidding into an angle that was almost a laydown, Nick gained on the kid and squeezed him against a wire mesh fence that ran the length of a playground. At the speed they were going, the kid had a quick decision to make: give in or go down. All balls and no brains, he still had some vestige of the old self-preservation instinct, and at the last possible second he pulled back, as Nick whizzed past him with an inch or so to spare between them. He cut over and through an opening in the fence.

He looked back; the kid had crashed after all. Nick waited while he righted his bike and climbed back on. He came up to Nick.

"You're a real fucking wacko, you know that?" the kid snarled. He looked like he was going to either cry or kill somebody.

"Just give me the money, pal," Nick said nicely.

2

*T*he El Greco diner was really a hangar-size road-house, and when Nick opened the door, some of the cold air came in with him. At three o'clock in the afternoon there was only one customer at the counter, a terrific-looking redhead sipping on a tall drink. Nick slid himself onto a stool two or three down from her.

"Hi, Dewey." He greeted the counterman. "How are you doing? Shit, it's cold." He turned to the redhead. "Hi," he tried on her.

"Hi," she said, pleasantly enough.

"Smells good in here," Nick told Dewey. "Got a coffee?"

Dewey drew one from the huge percolator and set it in front of him. The mug was thick and white, and the coffee tasted real. "Thanks, pal," Nick said. He took a slim flask from his inside jacket pocket and poured a shot into the coffee. Then he turned to offer some to the redhead. She shook her head: no, thanks.

"I'll bet I can tell what kind of perfume you're wearing," he said.

"Oh, really? Think so?" She thought it over for a second. "So what kind of perfume am I wearing?"

Nick inhaled deeply. He pretended to analyze the air for a minute and then he proclaimed, "Smells like trouble."

"You're right," she said. "That's exactly what I'm wearing."

"And I'll bet— Nah, I'd better not. Never mind."

"What?"

"No, I can't say it."

"Yeah, you can."

"Well," he drawled, spinning on his stool to look at her squarely. She had a full sensuous mouth, and the red hair was real. His kind of lady. "I bet I can guess what kind of underwear you're wearing. Based on your perfume."

"Really? That's pretty good."

Nick took a slug of the hearty coffee and waited. She didn't think about it too long. "All right. What kind of underwear am I wearing?"

"I can't hear you," Nick said.

"I said *what kind of underwear am I wearing?*"

Nick grinned. "None," he declared.

She laughed. "You're absolutely right."

And then she cracked up laughing, and Nick got up and went over and put his arms around her and hugged her, and she hugged him back, and then he kissed her hard, and she kissed him too.

"Nicky, that's good," she said when they came up for air.

"The best," he agreed. "Dewey, she's the best."

"That's what you always tell me," the counterman acknowledged.

"Hungry?" Nick asked her.

She shook her head no. Nick put some money on the counter and grabbed her coat from a nearby hook. "Come on," he said impatiently, "let's get out of here."

Connie opened the seat bag and took out the spare helmet, fastened it under her chin, and climbed on behind him. It was only a few blocks—his apartment was in the East Village, her job was in the West Village, and the El Greco was somewhere in the middle. In a few minutes they pulled up in front of his building and walked down to his basement, which the joker landlord called a loft.

They headed straight for the bed, which was rumpled and hadn't been changed for maybe weeks, but was very inviting, somehow. They fell onto the bed and were enveloped in its warmth. It was true, she wasn't wearing any.

The room darkened as the afternoon moved on into early winter night. Connie looked at the clock, finally, and groaned. She sat up and reached for her skirt. It had fallen on the floor alongside his last several days' worth of clothes. She sat on the edge of the bed to dress while Nick watched her lazily from under the covers.

"You're pretty," he said.

"Thanks."

"Pretty sensational."

She didn't smile. Something on her mind. He waited for her to say it, whatever it was. "You going to race tonight?" she asked.

"Yeah."

He waited and she put on her blouse, buttoned it, reached for her sweater, and pulled it over her head. She looked at him. He didn't say anything.

"Two men came round the hospital asking about you," she said finally.

"Cops?" Nick asked quickly.

Connie looked unhappy. She reached into her bag and found a hairbrush. "They didn't have it written on their heads in grease pencil, but I'm familiar with the type," she said.

Nick was thoughtful. Unnerved, in fact.

Connie pulled the brush through her hair angrily. Nick didn't say anything, and she finally broke the silence. "So? What are we supposed to talk about? Perfume?" She threw the brush back into her purse and stood up. She poked her foot around the piles of clothes and newspapers until she found her shoes and slipped into them.

"Connie . . ." But he didn't know what else to say.

She shrugged into her coat. "It's getting too cold, even for me, Nicky," she said. "I don't think I want to do this anymore." She was sad. So was he. She waited for him to say something, but there wasn't anything to say. She walked toward the door and stopped, but she didn't turn around, and when he didn't say anything, she left. Maybe she didn't mean it to, but the door slammed, hard.

Nick lay there staring at the pipes and conduits that passed for decoration in his basement apartment. Everything was gray, painted that color a long time ago and then enhanced with crud and dust and grime over the years. He got out of bed and headed for the kitchen area, skirting around the center of the room where parts of another Harley were laid out on a dropcloth.

He found the telephone and the answering machine under last Sunday's newspaper. The little red light was flashing and the digital readout said: two messages. He flicked the playback switch.

"Nick, are you there? . . . Pick up, would you? . . . I know you're there . . ."

That was the trouble—she had never trusted him. He hadn't been there, but she was so sure he was. She thought he lied all the time, but he didn't. He hadn't. He opened the refrigerator door, careful not to dislodge the brightly colored finger paintings that were stuck all over it, and took out a can of beer. He pulled back the tab and sipped at it as he slid down, still bare-assed, along the side of the cold fridge till he was sitting on the floor. Her voice still had the power to reduce him to this.

". . . I'm taking the kids to my mom this Saturday . . . You can have them the following Saturday . . . The school called. We're behind another month— that makes three, and . . . and it's winter, you know, they need new coats and—"

Nick reached up over his head and flicked off the machine. He sat motionless for a minute, his forehead against the unyielding enamel. He reached up to peel off a finger painting, careful not to tear it. He smiled, looking at it, and then he lost his smile as he looked around the basement, furnished with haphazard purchases from discount stores and friends' garages. Except for the children's paintings, everything around him was drab and depressing.

Some apartment. Some life.

So what are you going to do, sit here stone naked

feeling sorry for yourself and maybe cry a little? Going in for self-pity now, are we? Fuck that. He got up off the floor, wet the back of the painting to reactivate the flour-and-water paste, replaced it on the fridge door, and listened to the rest of the message while he dressed.

His ex-wife finally ran out of troubles, and then the second message started. Inspector Richard Crown would be expecting him at precinct headquarters on Monday at 9 A.M. sharp. He could bring his lawyer with him if he wished.

3

*R*ounding a corner near the precinct house, Nick spotted Charlie Vincent standing on the curb waiting for the light to change. Charlie was duded up in a suit that was too much—too wide at the shoulders, too narrow on the hips. He was a character, young Charlie, out from the ghetto with both fists flying, determined to make something of himself. Nick liked Charlie Vincent as much as any cop he'd ever met.

He swerved the Harley to a stop, and Charlie hopped right on behind him. He stuck his feet straight out on either side of Nick, like a kid on a merry-go-round steed.

"What do you see?" Charlie hollered in his ear as Nick gunned up and started off with a roar.

Nick had to laugh. "A Guido in a suit they should pay you to wear!" he yelled back over his shoulder.

"Some detective," Charlie complained loudly. He

wagged his feet in the air and Nick looked down at a shiny new shoe. "Bostonians!" Charlie shouted. "Eighty-five bucks! Girls go for shoes, it's the second place they look."

Nick hooted and shook his head. His long hair went flying; some of it got in Charlie's face. "Hey, I read about it in a magazine!" the cop protested.

They took a corner onto the crosstown street where the precinct house stood rimmed with police cars, marked and unmarked. It was the middle of a shift change and a fresh tour of uniforms was hitting the street.

Charlie lowered his voice and leaned forward to talk right into Nick's ear. "When Internal Affairs comes to your office, it's not as bad as making you come to them, is it?"

Nick shrugged. "I'll let you know. It's my first house call." He slowed the bike on the approach to the precinct house.

"Hey, why don't you just dazzle the bastards? Go in uniform," Charlie suggested. Nick turned his head for a skeptical glance back at his passenger.

"I mean it," Charlie insisted. He was an earnest young kid, still in his middle twenties, eager and damp-eared. "Sure, let them see your breast bars," he went on, lowering his voice as they came to a stop. The street in front of the station was suddenly filling with uniforms. "Hey, a detective like you, with commendations up the wazoo? Hell, they should name a wing in Attica after you!"

Nick was grinning as he pulled into a parking spot.

"Hey, Vincent!"

They looked up. A burly scowling cop carrying thirty pounds of excess flab was coming out of the station house, and calling to Charlie as if he owned him. Maybe he didn't like the company Charlie Vincent was keeping. "Hey, come on, off and on! Let's go!" the cop barked.

Charlie slid down from the Harley with deliberately slow movements. He stood and looked over at the cop as if weighing whether to hop to it or run over and break the guy's nose. Charlie would never do that; he was not a violent guy. He had grown up—or as much as he had time for—in a good family in a bad neighborhood, and he was a whole lot tougher than his boyish good looks made him out to be.

"Grab your dick, Farentino, and count to infinity!" he yelled back. That took care of that. He turned to Nick. "I'll meet you at Scalari's for lunch. On me. We'll have a party and a half."

Nick had heavy stuff on his mind. He looked up at the front door of the precinct house. "I'll think about it, hot dog," he said.

Charlie backed away, toward Farentino and a couple of other uglies who were waiting for him. "Yo, Conklin," Charlie called back to Nick. "You don't show, you'll be in real trouble. Thirteen hundred." He gestured up to the upper reaches of the building. "Watch your tail, cowboy."

Hero worship, sort of—the kid was young and mostly untried. He still liked tough guys, and Nick Conklin was real, real tough. Yeah. So how come his stomach was dropping a stitch as he climbed the stairs?

Nick walked into the locker room. There were a lot of cops in there, hurrying to get out on the street or just weary and grateful that they'd made it through another night. Some eyes glanced over at Nick but seemed not to see him. No one said a word to him. But suddenly a steel hand grabbed his sleeve and he was looking squarely into one of the reddest, maddest, most threatening faces it had been his lifelong privilege to meet. It was the precinct captain, Jim Oliver, dressed in a rumpled brown pinstriped civilian suit that did nothing for him.

"You'll walk if you tell the truth and keep your wits," he was told. The other cops in the immediate area quieted down to listen. "Run your mouth and they'll screw you."

"I got nothing to hide," Nick said evenly. He shook himself free from the captain's grip.

Oliver wouldn't be shaken off that easily. "I hope not—for my sake. How's your lawyer?"

Nick shrugged. "I don't know him real well," he admitted.

Oliver waggled his white mustache in sympathy— mostly for himself, some for Nick. "If these people get their way, you'll get to know him real well," he predicted dolefully. "You'll probably be sending his kids through college."

It was his way of expressing sympathy, maybe, but it didn't help the knots in Nick's gut. Fuck, let's get it over with, Nick thought. He took his I.D. badge out of his wallet and clipped it to his sweater.

"Don't let the bastards make you sweat," the captain said, by way of encouragement.

"Nothing to sweat about," Nick reassured him, loudly enough for all the guys still hanging around the locker room to hear. Leaving that room felt like walking out of a pressure cooker. Yeah—into a microwave oven.

The lawyer Nick had hired by phone on his ex-brother-in-law's recommendation was already in the conference room with the investigators when Nick walked in. It was clearly going to be the old game of good cop/bad cop. Berg was the good news, at least he looked relatively human. He was sitting at one end of the long pockmarked conference table, flipping through what was obviously Nick's file. Berg was the younger of the two investigators, maybe not out of his thirties yet. His tie was already askew and his white shirt-sleeves were rolled up. He had a pleasant, sunny face, and horn-rimmed glasses. He looked up from the file and smiled with courtesy, if not exactly warmth, when Nick came in the room.

Nick's lawyer pulled out a chair next to his own for Nick. For one minute Nick couldn't remember his lawyer's name, but then it came to him: Yudell. Something Yudell—Marvin? Robert? Henry? What the fuck was the difference?

As soon as Nick had sat down, Berg said, "You're, ah . . . this is quite an impressive record." He said it with a lot of sincere-sounding respect. It was supposed to put Nick at ease, off-guard, even.

Investigator Crown was the bad news—sitting at the far end of the table, scowling and silent. He had never stopped wearing his hair in military white-walls, probably looked back on 'Nam as the best years of his life. Crown sat with his arms folded across his barrel chest, eyeing Nick as if he expected him to try to hook his watch. When he spoke, his voice was flat.

"Yeah, a regular hero."

There was an uncomfortable silence.

"Tell me about Monte Ronan," Crown said abruptly. He didn't work from notes, nor—apparently—from anything so cumbersome as an open mind.

Nick answered calmly. So far, no surprises. "He's a good man," he said. "The kind of cop you want watching your back when the shit falls in buckets."

Berg seemed to be digesting this, and Yudell sat silent, but Crown snorted in disgust.

"That's what you think?" he asked sarcastically.

"That's what I think," Nick repeated.

"He's dirt and you know it," Crown snarled.

Nick felt himself go tense and it must have showed. The lawyer looked sideways at him, a reminder more than an actual warning. Stay calm, above all don't lose your credibility.

"Where do you get your information, the nurses at St. Vincent's?" Nick said, turning it into almost a joke. Mild, but it got a little bile out of his stomach and he felt better for it.

Crown leaned forward slightly. In for the kill. "Tell us about Patrick Dunleavy," he said.

Before Nick could open his mouth, the lawyer jumped in. "My client has no knowledge of any malfeasance on the part of this officer . . ."

"Your client is in a good position to know," Crown insisted. He looked down the length of the table at Berg, who started riffling through the file in front of him until he found what he needed.

"Twenty-eight, June, eighty-eight. Your unit arrested three suspects," he read. "The cash was logged in at sixty-five thousand and change. We have reason to believe there was over seventy-three thousand in the vehicle you impounded." Berg looked up at Nick almost apologetically.

"Says who?" Nick erupted angrily.

"There are sources," Crown said.

"Meaning a suspect's word is better than a cop's?"

"Depends on the cop," Crown told him. The ex-marine settled back in his chair again. "I don't like heroes, Conklin. They think the rules don't apply to them."

"I'm clean," Nick said quietly.

Good-guy Berg took the ball and started dribbling. He was still reading from the thick file in front of him. "Well, Detective," he said, "you have—ah . . . a couple of kids at St. John's . . . house payments, alimony, an apartment. I'd say that was a king-size nut. I have to admire your thrift."

"That's everybody's life story," Nick told him. His tone of voice let Berg know exactly where he stood with this kind of shit.

"We did the math, hero," Crown said scornfully. "You're at least a thousand a month in the hole. You're into the Shylocks. You're taking."

Nick started to sweat. He half-rose from the chair. "If you want to run up a charge, go ahead," he said tersely. "If not, go piss on someone else."

"Nick . . ." Yudell interrupted. He didn't get a chance to say any more.

"We'll charge you," Crown told him savagely. "Someone will help us out. Nobody's got a softer center than a dirty cop."

Nick was doing his best to control himself.

In his mild heck-I'm-just-one-of-the-frat-boys voice, Berg cut in. "You could talk to us," he said, "or we can talk to the wife. What time do the kids get home?"

Nick sprang out of his chair and grabbed Berg's clean white collar, tightly enough so that the nice-guy look turned into one of sheer panic.

"Nick!" yelled his lawyer.

"You go near my family, I'll fall on you," Nick told the young smartass, face-to-face so he could hear every word.

"Are you threatening me, Detective?" Berg croaked.

"Nick, for God's sake!" Yudell yelled. This time Nick heard him. Staring into Berg's big blues for a tense beat, he opened his fists and let the bastard drop back into his chair.

Yudell was all wound up. "That's it!" he shouted. "We're through! My client will not tolerate any more harassment!"

Berg coughed and, with a look down the table at Crown, closed Nick's file. Yudell grabbed his briefcase and stood up, waiting for Nick. They were out of there in no time at all.

Nick headed for Scalari's. He could use a friend about now, not to mention a beer. The jukebox was playing Sinatra and the low-key scents of tomato sauce and homemade pasta were more soothing than a cool hand on your fevered brow. The fat twin Scalari brothers were behind the bar, Carmine pouring drinks and Pasquale working the deep fryer. Charlie Vincent sat at the bar, munching on fried calamari and marking up an *Arco Sergeants'* exam-review book with a yellow highlighter.

Nick slid onto the stool next to him and took a look over his shoulder. "Civil rights, civil procedure? Boy, they make it tough these days, don't they. You studying for Sergeant or Supreme Court Justice?"

Charlie sized him up fast. Wilted at the edges, and more than just weary. They must have really leaned on him. But he was here, and that was something.

"Have a beer?" Charlie offered.

Nick pointed at the open book. "Is this really necessary?"

Charlie nodded. "If you want the braid, you gotta know the stuff," he said.

"Time was all you had to know was the right councilman. Scotch on the rocks," he told Carmine.

Charlie shut the book. "You drinking Scotch? It must have really gone bad with the shooflies."

"Well, there's no home-court advantage, I can tell you that much."

"Bastards got their job, I guess."

Nick looked at him, not quite sure about—what? Something. "It's a great place to be if you want up and into headquarters," he said.

It was clear on Charlie's face that he couldn't believe Nick would suspect him. "Oh, man . . ." he started to say, and then stopped, and started to unbutton his shirt. "Excuse me," he said. "Please talk into my left tit. Me and Carmine here, we're both wired. If we bump into each other the lights dim."

Nick laughed. He waved Charlie off. "I'm just seeing devils in the bean dip," he said by way of apology. "I'm way out of line."

"No shit," said Charlie. "Forget it."

Nick took a long slug of Scotch and felt the muscles in his neck unknot. He relaxed and glanced down the bar. "Two of Frankie Abolafia's goons down at the end there," he noted.

"Oh, yeah, the Capo's here, came in just before you did. Keeping some strange company."

"Where?" asked Nick without turning around.

"Two tables over in a direct line with the goons," Charlie told him, also without looking.

Nick glanced around the room casually and almost choked on his Scotch. "I'll say strange! What the hell is the Wolf doing with a couple of Buddha heads?"

"Maybe the mob wants to start driving Subarus," Charlie chuckled.

"Oh, well, a lot of Japanese like Pasquale's cooking —look around, they come here in droves. Why not? I could even go for some of it myself."

"You're on," Charlie said. As he reached in his pocket to leave some money on the bar, he took another glance over at the mobster's table.

"I make the young Jap as the translator," Charlie speculated. "But—what the hell, right? Not our beat."

The usual lunchtime crowd was filling the place now but there was something eye-catching about the customers who came through the door just then. Two Japanese men, moving just furtively enough to attract attention, came in together and cased the room, moving apart to make room for a third man, sporting heavy sun shades which he neglected to take off as he came in from the street. He was about forty, with spiky black hair, dressed in a very expensive dark suit with a cashmere coat thrown over his shoulders. Obviously the Boss Man of this weird trio.

Before he could say anything to Charlie, the first man pulled a uzi out from under his coat and stood in front of the door holding it up for all to see. The second goon strode to the center of the restaurant and withdrew his own weapon of the same make, shouting a single word of command in Japanese: *"Gogona!"* The guns pointed slowly around the room, restless and ready.

"What's going on?" One of Abolafia's men at the

bar muttered. He was half on his feet and quivering with tension. One of the scatterguns instantly turned toward him.

"Relax," his boss ordered quickly. "Calm down."

The bodyguard sat back down warily and the gunman started slowly scanning the room again, in case anybody got any ideas. In the back of the room, a woman moaned with fear and was quickly hushed by her companion.

The tension in the room was as thick as the spaghetti sauce. Suddenly Nick was aware of a slight movement at his side. Charlie was inching his weapon from its holster, sliding it carefully into his right hand under the lip of the bar.

"Don't think about it," Nick whispered urgently. "Don't think about it."

"It's done, babe," Charlie whispered back.

The gutsy damned fool was going to get himself killed one of these days.

4

*T*he man with the shades and spiky hair walked slowly toward the table where the Italian *Capo* was sitting with his two unlikely companions.

The older Japanese man at Abolafia's table clearly recognized his countryman as he approached the table. Contempt was written all over his face as he spat out the intruder's name.

"Sato." He made it sound like he'd swallowed a bad clam.

The man in the sunglasses stepped up close to the table. Instinctively, the two heavies at the end of the bar leaned forward, fists clenched, but just as quickly, their boss made a tiny motion with his hand and they sat back. Abolafia had put enough people into similar situations to be philosophical about what was about to happen. It was not his or his family's business. He was personally in no danger. His bodyguards could stay out of it.

The men with the uzis held everyone in thrall as Sato leaned over the table to open the older man's silk-lined suit jacket. A flat package protruded from the inside left breast pocket. Sato removed the package and tore at the wrapping. He threw the bright yellow paper scornfully at the terrified young translator.

Abolafia shoveled up a forkful of pasta. He was the only patron in the entire restaurant eating. Why let good food go cold?

Sato was apparently satisfied with what he found in the package. He fitted the wooden lid back onto the flat narrow box. He turned to walk away from the table.

The young translator called out something to him in Japanese, some insult which could not be ignored. It was foolish of him. Sato handed the long flat box to one of his gunmen. He put his hands in his pockets and walked back to the table. He withdrew his hand with a gleaming *tanto* knife in it, and with one thrust, buried the blade deep into the man's chest. He withdrew it with a half-twist, and in the same motion brought the dagger up and to the left to slash the throat of the older man. His blood gushed over the table before the translator had hit the floor.

Abolafia took another mouthful of pasta and washed it down with a giant gulp of wine. "You people are wild . . . wild," he said, meaning it as a compliment.

Sato picked up a napkin. Tenderly wiping the blood from his *tanto,* he strolled toward the front door. As he left, the gunman at the door turned to follow him. After a moment the second thug waved his scattergun once more across the room and turned to go out.

Nick had been sitting absolutely silent and apparently as paralyzed as everyone else in the room, but the instant the gunman turned his back, Nick had his Colt Airweight in hand and was after him.

"Call 911," Charlie shouted at Carmine. "Get backup!"

Nick stopped in the foyer with his gun drawn and called out to the gunman's back. "Police!" he yelled. "Hold it right there!"

The uzi spat as the man spun around wildly. Nick dropped to his knees and got off one shot; the gunman crashed forward through the front door onto the pavement outside. Nick bolted out after him, leaping over the man's body in pursuit of bigger game.

Outside, the bright sunlight hit Nick head on. As Nick flew out of Scalari's and hit the ground, he saw Sato disappearing into the passenger side of a waiting Lincoln whose driver was already gunning the accelerator. The front door slammed as the car took off; Nick saw the other guy in the back—the man with the second uzi. He was aiming it at Nick, but Nick got him first, right through the head.

Then he emptied his Colt at the speeding black Lincoln and managed to take at least two direct bites out of it. The rear window shattered and it looked like the driver took a hit to the head, but by then it was a block away and still moving.

Out of control, the Lincoln swerved in front of an oncoming truck. There was one hell of a crash and the crumpled truck came to a stop, blocking Nick's view. He took off on foot, reloading with his speedloader as he ran.

Charlie came tearing out of Scalari's with his gun drawn, but the street was empty. In the distance, coming closer, sirens started to rise like the cavalry charge in an old movie.

"Nick!" Charlie yelled. He stared down the street. "Shit! Shit!"

Nick came around the crashed truck in time to see Sato and his surviving henchman running in opposite directions. Nick stayed with the killer, who was heading around the corner toward the river, onto Little West 12th Street.

It was the old wholesale meat market district, and the cobblestones were slippery, wet with blood and water from the hoses that constantly washed it off. The street was jammed with trucks of all sizes and descriptions, and workers in bloodstained white jackets, like doctors.

Row after row of butchered cattle hung from ceiling hooks, making a ghoulish kind of ceiling for this busy work area. Workers were sliding gigantic slabs of raw meat from the backs of refrigerator trucks while others loaded them into the meat lockers and secured them to hooks.

Sato ducked into one of the dozens of meat lockers that lined the arcaded buildings. Nick was right behind him, dodging men unloading sides of beef, whole calves, and crates of decapitated chickens.

Before entering the locker he tried to clear the civilians out of harm's way. "Police!" he yelled to the workers who were standing around gawking. "Get the fuck out of here," he told them.

Inside, Sato walked through the crowd of workers as if he belonged there, custom-made suit and all. With his gun drawn, Nick had to be more cautious. "Police!" he repeated. "Get the fuck out of here. The guy who just came through—where did he go? Now, get out! You, out! You can get hurt, get the fuck out! out! Where did he go? Get outta here!"

They suddenly got the message, and in another minute the place was as cleaned as a plucked chicken. Now there was only Nick—and a half-flight of wooden stairs leading to the refrigerated area. He started up after Sato.

Rows and rows of slabs of beef hung from the overhead racks. Nick picked his way cautiously, trying not to crash head on with the swinging tons of dead meat. Down one row he saw some carcasses swaying. Something had set them in motion—deliberately? He moved slowly down the aisle.

Standing on a pile of cartons behind an enormous side of beef, holding a plastic bag inverted high in the air, Sato let Nick get past him. As Nick crept into the trap, Sato brought the bag down over Nick's head.

Nick fired the Colt but he was blinded by the smothering plastic and his shot went wild, deep into somebody's future T-bone steak. Before Nick's reflexes could get him out of the way, his wrist was kicked sharply by the toe of a Versace shoe and the Colt went flying out of his hand as he fell backward over the stack of boxes. He ripped the plastic bag from his face.

As his vision cleared he saw something suddenly glint in front of him, catching the light with a flashing movement. Sato materialized in front of him holding his *tanto* high in the air.

The fight was fast, close, and mean. Nick grabbed Sato's arm and delivered a roundhouse punch to the man's jaw. He thought he heard some teeth crunching, but it didn't slow Sato down. He kicked into Nick's stomach with those hand-made shoes, and Nick went down in agony. Sato cocked his leg for another kick, but Nick managed to scissor the business-suited legs out from under him. Nick stayed close to the ground as Sato rolled away.

As they moved together again warily, each ready for the kill, Sato's knife streaked through the air and slashed down through the flesh and brow over Nick's right eye.

Blood poured down to blind him in that eye but it only made Nick madder. He had a lifetime of New York street fighting behind him. As for Sato, he was highly trained in the martial arts, and he had the weapon. This could go either way.

Nick dodged a few more swipes of the knife and as Sato leaned into a particularly vicious jab, Nick caught him off balance and pulled him down. Sato fell on top of him and they began wrestling for the knife.

Feet pounded up the stairs—a load of cops, with weapons leveled. Charlie Vincent was in front, impatient as hell. He ran up and jammed his gun into Sato's ribs.

"You feel this. You see me. You see me!" he shouted wildly. Another cop twisted Sato's wrist until he dropped the knife. Nick shoved Sato off him and started to get up. The cops pulled Sato to his feet. Nick was reaching under a couple of tons of beef to retrieve his Colt when Sato got off one final kick right into his kidneys.

Before Nick could retaliate, the cops piled on and overpowered Sato. He quit struggling, but when his eyes met Nick's there was a promise in them.

5

*T*he captain was so eager to know what the hell was going on that he met them at the door of the precinct house. They walked down the hall together toward the bullpen: Nick with a painful limp and Charlie trying not to help him and Captain Oliver asking questions a mile a minute.

"This package the guy was after, can you describe?"

"Looked like a smooth dark wood, high grade, polished. Flat, thin, about—" Nick outlined the narrow wooden box with his hands. "About this by this," he said. "Maybe five by seven-or-ten inches." His side hurt where Sato had kicked him.

"Dope?" asked Oliver.

Nick shook his head. That made his eye hurt where it had been slashed right through the brow. "Not in that company," he said.

"So what warranted the big shitstorm?" Oliver was puzzled. He slowed his stride to accommodate Nick.

"Could be anything," Charlie said.

They passed an interrogation room with its door wide open. Glancing inside, Nick saw "Wolf" Abolafia with his Park Avenue lawyer and two officers having a civilized conversation. That is, the attorney and the detectives seemed to be having words; just looking at them you knew "Wolf" hadn't said a single word since "get my lawyer" and wasn't about to.

"What's his version?" Nick asked as they walked on past the open door.

"He's a poor citizen whose lunch was interrupted," Oliver said.

"He must be hungry," Charlie said.

"Come to think of it—" Nick said.

Charlie snapped his fingers. "I knew I forgot something."

The captain looked at them without appreciation for the wit. "I'm dying to know what you people were doing in a joint full of wiseguys," he said dryly.

Charlie was about to answer but Nick cut him off. "There's nothing in the patrol guide about where and what to eat, Cap."

Oliver put his hand on the doorknob of the bullpen, but before he opened it he turned to Nick and said, quietly, "I would think someone in your position would want to keep his head down."

They followed him past desks piled with paperwork and cops poring over it. Nick glanced down at a desk featuring eight-by-ten black-and-white glossies of last night's corpses laid out on autopsy tables. A detective was shuffling them, apparently looking for someone or something.

They stopped at a table that was covered with evidence from the recent massacre: shell casings, receipts, weapons, bloodstained napkins from Scalari's . . . it was all being catalogued and carefully boxed by a young cop wearing skin-tight plastic gloves.

Nick picked up a shell casing, turned it over thoughtfully, and set it back down.

"The Bureau is sending a guy down to find out what the Jap mob and the Mafia were doing sharing a bottle of Chianti," the captain said.

"So nobody knows anything," Charlie mused aloud.

"Right," the captain agreed.

"Is there a tap on Abolafia?" Nick asked.

Oliver nearly smiled. "The last time that joker talked on a clear phone, calls were a nickel," he said.

Nick picked up a plastic bag that held scraps of torn yellow paper. "This is what the package was wrapped in," he told Oliver.

The captain nodded. "Okay, get it to the lab on the morning pouch and then try the borough. Don't bet your sock money, though."

Nick nodded and turned away from the evidence table. There was nothing else he could do here, not at this point, anyway. There was someone who could help, though, and Nick was dying to open him up.

"Where's my darling?" he asked. The captain nodded and turned on his heel to lead the way. Charlie and Nick followed him without saying much until they reached Interrogation Room #3. The door was shut—not that anyone could have learned anything from what was going on inside. The captain led them into an observation room next door, where they could watch through one-way glass. Sato was sitting ramrod-straight, his tie all neat and straight again, the blood-stains on his shirt quite dry and his mouth firmly shut. A detective was sitting opposite him, tossing out questions which were being translated by a Japanese-American interpreter. Just inside the door stood another Japanese man, impeccably dressed in the standard-issue uniform of expensive dark suit, white shirt, and solid-citizen tie.

"He doesn't speak a word of English," Oliver said glumly. "But he won't speak Japanese, either."

"It's my collar," Nick said, "my case."

Oliver gestured toward the stiff figure standing at the door. "Japanese embassy. They want him first."

"What?" Nick sputtered.

"Listen, Nick, while you were in the emergency room getting stitched up, there were enough strings pulled by enough politicians in Japan to fly ten thousand kites. I don't know why, but this dozo is important. They want him back home, real bad."

Nick was enraged. "Captain," he said, controlling it nicely, "I've got three people's blood on my clothes, and some of it is mine. I got two clean homicide convictions here. Witnesses, the works. They can have him back—in twenty to life."

Oliver had been carrying a manila envelope under his arm. Now he handed it to Nick.

"What's this?" Nick opened the envelope and pulled out a pair of airline tickets, a stack of vouchers, and a wad of cash.

"The Japanese embassy talked to the State Department," Oliver told him wearily. "Then State talked to Police Plaza. They talked to me and I'm talking to you. Shit rolls downhill. They want someone to take him back. That's you and Vincent here. They say you haven't lived till you've seen Mount Fuji."

Nick stared at him, wondering what the gag was. "This is bullshit, Captain," he said. He could feel his anger rising again. His mouth became a tight line as he fought himself for control.

Conklin was leaning toward insubordination, but Oliver let it slide. "You want Internal Affairs to keep hammering you?" he asked. "From what I hear, you already went off in their faces, which is exactly what they like. Take a breather. Do us both a favor. Have a nice trip."

Oliver headed for the door. Before he got out, Nick called out to him. "Hey . . ." The captain turned around, waiting. Nick reached into his pocket and pulled out a ring of keys. He tossed them to Oliver, who caught them on reflex, looking puzzled. "As long as Internal Affairs is going to be in my apartment," Nick said, "tell them to water the plants."

Captain Oliver was not amused. He dropped Nick's keys on a table by the door. "I'll back you up a hundred percent, Nick," he said, "as long as you're right." He left the room. Nick picked up the wad of cash, counted it, peeled off some and put it in his wallet. He put the rest back in the manila envelope.

He turned to meet Charlie's quizzical eye, and Charlie immediately broke out in a sheepish grin, maybe for what he was thinking, maybe for what he was about to say. "Gee, Japan, how bad can it be? They say the geisha girls train all their lives for it, do you think that's true?"

"I guess we're going to find out," Nick said absently, turning to take another long look at Sato through the glass.

He still sat straight as a sword on the hard chair, with his mouth tightly shut. The detective was running out of patience, but Sato didn't respond to him or to the imprecations of the earnest young translator. The official from the embassy stood silently, watching and listening and waiting.

Abruptly, Sato half-turned in his chair to look up at the mirror. Although Sato couldn't possibly see Nick through the one-way glass, he somehow, uncannily, seemed to know Nick was there watching him. Sato made a cutting motion across his forehead, over his right eye, in the exact spot where Nick's bandage covered the cut the *tanto* had inflicted.

It was weird, a little unsettling. But it was all over between them, wasn't it? Nick had to babysit his own collar all the way to Japan and turn him over to somebody else, safe and sound, just hand him over, just like that. For what, he wondered? What had Sato done to make himself more wanted at home in his own country than he was right here and now by this lean and very hungry American cop?

Nick ran his fingers through his too-long hair. He looked at Charlie, who couldn't hide his excitement.

"You ever been out of New York before, Charlie?"

"Sure, Nick. I went to Jersey once. Saw a cow."

That was bullshit, because Charlie had been a scholarship student at one of the big important colleges in Boston. He was a nice kid, and what the hell, he'd be good company on the long boring flight.

6

*T*he Harley blasted across the 59th Street Bridge and onto Queens Boulevard against the early morning traffic coming into the city. Nick turned off onto a side street and slowed, keeping the noise level down to jibe with the quiet suburban neighborhood. He pulled up in front of a small, neat house that was going to need a paint job soon. He gave the motor two quick raps and got off the bike, waiting at the curb, his eye on the front door.

It was only a minute before the door opened, and he could see Peggy standing there. She didn't open the screen door, she didn't say a word. Neither did he. Nothing to say, anymore.

Suddenly two kids shot past her before she could slow them down or stop them. They were great-looking boys, with his dishwater-blond straight hair and Peggy's soft brown eyes. Patrick was eight and

Danny was ten, and they both had a bit of devil in them despite the trim gray trousers and blue blazers and ties they wore.

When he saw them, Nick's face lit up and he grinned like a kid himself—making the resemblance between himself and the boys suddenly apparent to anyone, if anyone had been looking. With the grimness gone, he was not a bad-looking guy: straight features, strong chin, intelligent gray eyes that just this minute were filled with love and pride.

"Dad!" Danny yelped excitedly, barreling straight down the walk and into Nick's outstretched arms. After a terrific hug, Danny's eagerness to tell his tale was more than he could contain. The words spilled out like tumbling blocks. "Patrick's in trouble! He called Sister Elizabeth a name and she heard!"

Patrick was scuffing his newly polished shoes along the walkway, taking as long as he could to join his father and brother. He carried an enormous bookpack on his back and seemed unfairly, sadly weighed down for such a little boy. Nick's heart thumped over.

"What'd he call her, Daniel?" he asked.

Danny grinned—Nick's grin and Nick's dad's grin, too. "An ugly goose!" he announced with delight.

Nick looked horrified and clasped his hands over his ears. He looked back at Patrick, who was standing quite still a few feet away, his head down. Nick lowered his voice conspiratorially. "Hey, Patrick? I always thought exactly the same thing. Don't tell her I said so, though."

Patrick looked at him levelly, with Peggy's eyes.

"Hey, guess what, gang? You'll never guess in a million years where I have to go today."

"Far?" Patrick asked.

"Very far, but I'll be back here in just a few days."

"Brooklyn!" Danny guessed.

Patrick just looked at him, waiting.

"Do you know where Japan is?" Nick asked them, trying to put some enthusiasm behind it.

"Sure," Patrick said.

"Everybody knows that," Danny told him. "You going to Japan?"

"Yep."

"You going to bring me a Ninja sword?" Patrick asked, testing him, challenging him. They had split up when Patrick was too young to even know he had a father, and it showed, sometimes.

"I'll bring you something nice," Nick promised.

"A Ninja sword is nice," Patrick persisted.

"And Transformers," Danny chipped in. "They got the best ones."

"How about a ride to school?" Nick asked, pointing to the bike.

Patrick reached for his brother's hand. "Mom says it's not safe anymore."

But Danny was pulling away, toward the bike and his dad. "Let's go! I can get on by myself."

Nick glanced back at the house. Peggy was still standing there, watching them from inside the screen door.

He looked down at the two people he loved most in the world and he wondered, as he did every time, how he could stand to leave them. He hugged Danny's shoulders, and reached out for Patrick, who ducked. Nick just ruffled the soft yellow hair and let it go at that.

"Yeah, well, maybe your mom's right," he said. In

the face of Danny's disappointment, he said, "Well, you guys take care, okay? I'll see you as soon as I get back. Hey, I love you guys."

"Yeah, okay," Danny said. He let Patrick take his hand again.

"Bye," Patrick said.

"Bye," Nick said. He watched them go up the street and around the corner. Without looking back at the house, he reached for his wallet, emptied every bit of cash from it into the mailbox that still said CONKLIN. He jumped on the bike and took off in the opposite direction with a thunderous, deafening roar.

And there they were on a 747, a real jolly threesome: Charlie at the window, Nick on the aisle, and Sato between them with his cuffed hands on his lap. Charlie was reading a guidebook, all about Japan. Nick was playing solitaire, slapping the cards down on the tray in front of him glumly.

Charlie wished he could cheer him up. For him it was a terrific opportunity and even an adventure—how many members of the NYPD get trips to the Orient, all expenses paid? But of course he understood how Nick must be feeling. Sitting next to the guy you should be putting away could take the fun out of travel.

"Hey, Nick—you're the one who says you never go anywhere," he reminded his partner cheerily.

Nick raised one eyebrow. "I was thinking Vegas, Charlie. Reno, maybe."

Charlie shook his head. "What are you missing? Riding your motorcycle to some nurse's house. That shit is sadder than Ethiopia."

Nick kept right on playing solitaire.

With a burst of inspiration, Charlie put the guide-book down and leaned over Sato to light a little fire under Nick, maybe even cheer him up.

"Listen, Nick, it doesn't have to be just work, turn around and go back. Suppose I call and say I got the dreaded Asians from some raw clams and we stretch it into three days? You and me, we become a driving force on the local geisha scene . . ."

Nick almost smiled but he shook his head. "Not a prayer," he said firmly.

"Oh, come on." Charlie scoffed. "Big guy like you? New York cop? You're gonna be the biggest thing to hit this town since Godzilla."

Nick smiled. Satisfied, Charlie returned to his book. Through it all, Sato sat between them like a statue, unheeding.

"Hey, Nick, it says here that it's considered impolite to touch someone while you're talking to them."

Nick's arm brushed Sato's right off the armrest. "No shit," he said.

Charlie nudged Sato from the other side. "Guess that means you can't talk and screw at the same time. Right, hot dog?" Sato sat immobile, staring straight ahead. "What's the matter?" Charlie asked him. "No habla the English? Comprendo this, Tyrone: you will never fuck with my partner again. Get that?"

"Look at him," Nick said. "All piss and attitude." He looked away in disgust. "What do you think it's costing to take this beauty home?" he speculated.

Charlie put his nose back in his book. "It's not worth the cost of the dirt to bury him," he said.

Nick nodded thoughtfully. "A cop like Ronan puts

his ass on the line fourteen hours a day for years so he can spend the rest of his life in debt." He reached a hand over to run a deliberate finger down the lapel of Sato's impeccable hand-tailored suit. "This bastard's wearing my house payment."

Sato looked straight ahead. Maybe he was meditating.

Charlie's decent face took on a sad cast. His dark eyes were troubled. "People get desperate," he said slowly. "People get tempted. That doesn't make them less wrong."

Nick shook his head angrily. "Dead wrong," he said. "If Ronan took a little off the top from some dealer and locked him up in the bargain, he shouldn't get crucified. You don't have a family. Maybe his kids need braces, a better school—who the fuck knows. He's just trying to get by, not go to the fucking Riviera."

Suddenly Sato's eyes flicked over to Nick. He had caught something in the tone of voice, maybe—something that made him think Nick was close to losing it, maybe.

It made Nick crazy. "What the fuck are you looking at?" he shouted, half-rising from his seat.

Charlie spoke quickly. "Stay down, Nicky, all right?"

Nick pulled back. Sato stared ahead again, but a tiny smile had passed over his lips. Nick leaned back in his seat again and tried to calm himself by figuring what the penalty might be for murdering a collar with your bare hands while en route to delivering him for extradition.

They had dinner, and then Charlie took Sato to the

lav, and then the cabin lights were lowered for a movie featuring thirteenth-century Japanese *samurai* warriors grunting at each other. Those with earphones could select an audio channel in either English or Japanese. Charlie and Nick chose neither; Sato was not consulted.

Charlie napped. Nick dealt himself another hand of solitaire. He laid five cards out in a row, facedown. As he was contemplating which to turn over, Sato surprised him by looking over and then reaching to turn one of the cards. It was a winner.

Sato smiled, a wide grin showing large uneven teeth. Nick smiled back. Then he elbowed Sato in the ribs, hard. Sato bent over in pain. His inadvertent grunt woke Charlie.

"What happened?" Charlie asked, instantly alert. He looked at Sato, who was holding his side with both cuffed hands. "What's the matter with him?"

Nick shrugged. He felt better than he had in a while. "I guess he didn't like the movie," he told Charlie.

Charlie went back to his dreams of geisha girls, and even Sato closed his eyes for a few hours, but Nick never slept on planes, trains, or anything else that was moving. The long night passed, finally, and indications of bright sunny skies beat against the shaded windows. When the cabin lights went on for breakfast service, Sato's eyes opened without expression. Charlie stretched and yawned and checked out the prisoner, then his partner.

"You okay?" he asked Nick.

"Sure."

"Get any sleep?"

"Sure."

Charlie cracked the shade, and brilliant sunlight flooded over them. "Hey, look!" he breathed, opening the view as widely as the window would permit. There was the top of Mount Fuji, snow-covered and rose-haloed, just like in the ads.

Nick nudged Sato. "Welcome home, darling," he said.

Sato stared out the window at the breathtaking sight of the sacred mountain, but you couldn't tell whether he was glad to see it or not.

The 747 glided down smoothly, and after an interminable wait, the passengers started to file out with their bags and coats in hand. Nick cuffed himself to Sato but he made no move to get up from his aisle seat. Charlie stood up and moved his muscles in the cramped space. He peered out the window at Osaka Airport, or what he could see of it.

"No brass band . . . that's funny. No key to the city? Maybe they throw rice."

Sato tried to stand up, but Nick shoved him back down.

"Sit down, beautiful," he said. "You know something, Charlie, I'm not going to be sorry to be rid of this gonzo after all."

"Acts like he's in a rush to start his time, don't he?" Charlie commented.

"I kind of hope they're planning to hang him," Nick said dryly.

They sat still as the passengers continued to file out slowly. Then the galley hatch behind them opened from the outside, and a cleaning crew came on, followed by three officials, two in blue uniforms with brass buttons, the other in standard dark gray suit, white shirt, and dark tie. He was carrying a clipboard.

"Local heat," Nick said. "We're on."

He dug in his pocket for his badge and Charlie did the same; they hung them prominently on their jackets. Nick stood up, pulling Sato into the aisle with him.

The plainclothes cop spoke to them, bowing slightly. "Gentlemen, welcome to Japan. I am Inspector Nashida, Osaka Prefectural Police. Good flight?"

"Fabulous," Nick answered shortly. "I'm Conklin, this is Vincent. New York Police Department."

Charlie leaned forward to extend his hand to the inspector. "Charlie," he said, enunciating clearly. *"Konichi-wa."*

Nashida shook his hand and bowed. Charlie bowed back.

"I need to see the paperwork, Inspector," Nick snapped.

"Yes." Nashida nodded. He handed the clipboard and attached ballpoint pen to Nick. "Sign here, please . . . and here . . . and here . . ."

Nick looked down at a long piece of white paper covered in Japanese writing. "Nothing in English?" he asked.

"English?" Nashida repeated, bewildered. Apparently such an outlandish idea had never occurred to him. "No. Sorry," he added.

"Yeah . . . well . . ." Nick scrawled his name in all the places the inspector indicated.

Nashida tore off one of the carbon copies and

handed it back to Nick. "This is for you," he said. "Thank you so much for all your hard work." He bowed again, lower this time. Then he turned to bark at his two uniformed men. One of them pulled out a pistol.

Nick unfastened the cuffs. One of the Japanese cops yanked Sato aside unceremoniously. Sato was roughly searched and then cuffed.

"There is a driver outside Customs to take you to your hotel," Nashida informed Nick and Charlie. "Enjoy your stay in Osaka."

"Arigato," said Charlie. He grinned happily. "Take it slow, Inspector Nashida-san."

"Yeah, hurry back," Nick put in sardonically. "And here's one for you, Sato." He lifted his hand in an age-old salute, middle finger extended.

The inspector bowed again. Nick and Sato linked eyes for a moment, and then Sato was hustled out the galley hatch and down a ladder which had been raised to hatch level. Nashida brought up the rear of the little procession, and they made their way to a waiting, unmarked van.

"Yow-ee, let's go!" Charlie yelped happily. "We're off duty! I'm gonna be in and outta geishas like a Times Square pickpocket." He grabbed his bag and Nick grabbed his and they headed for the front of the plane.

"I'd settle for some shut-eye," Nick said.

"Sleep they got in New York, Nicky. What you want is action," said Charlie, making Nick feel about a hundred and ten years old. But he remembered when he was Charlie's age, and what the hell, it wasn't all that long ago. Maybe they should take a little R-and-R in Japan, why the hell not, as long as they were stuck here.

They headed down the aisle, toward the front of the plane where most of the passengers had already gotten off. A gorgeous flight attendant stood there saying goodbye and *sayonara,* and Charlie ogled her with frank appreciation. He lowered his voice. "Nick, did you know that each and every one of these dark-haired, small-assed contortionists is just waiting for a couple shields like us to make the birds sing?" As he passed the sexy young woman, he stopped in his tracks and bowed low. *"Domo arigato,"* he said. She smiled warmly at him.

"Where'd you get that bowing shit?" Nick asked him.

Charlie indicated his guidebook. "It's their country," he said.

"Giving you a book is like giving a baby a gun," Nick said disgustedly.

"Hey, when in Rome—"

"In Rome," interrupted Nick, "maybe I'll bow."

Just as they reached the front hatch, four Japanese policemen stepped through it into the plane. One of them eyed Nick and then dismissed him, looked on past him into the now-empty plane.

"Son of a bitch," Nick muttered.

The officer turned to him. "Detective Conklin?"

Nick and Charlie dropped their bags, grabbed their guns, and raced back up the aisle to the rear hatch, sending the cleaning crew flying out of their way.

They were just barely in time to see the van moving

out of the gate at the end of the tarmac. The rear window was open, and Sato was clearly visible, turned around to watch for them, laughing, with his finger up. He was audible, too.

"Raise you this, motherfucker!" he shouted, in what might be called perfect English.

7

*I*nstead of scooting down the service ladder, Nick took a flying-leap shortcut, landing on top of the cleaning truck which was pulled up to the loading hatch in the belly of the plane. The truck picked that moment to move out—in the opposite direction from Sato's van.

It was a while before his ridiculous predicament came to the attention of enough people along the route to get the driver's attention. When he stopped the truck and got out to see what everybody was yelling and pointing at, he ordered Nick down off the top of his truck in angry Japanese, much to the amusement of the airport workers who gathered from nowhere to watch the fun. Nick leaped down to the ground and made his way back to the terminal, where Charlie was already bowing and explaining as best he could to the real cops.

The bullpen of the Osaka police headquarters was different from any precinct HQ in the States only in the neatness of the desks. There was plenty of activity, and the usual number of desk jockeys going endlessly over piles of forms and reports and evidence. Computers clacked and phones rang, and over it all a shouting, New York–accented voice cut through everything.

"They had uniforms, and paperwork, Captain! It's not like I gave them cab fare," Nick screamed into the phone.

Nick was talking to his captain, who was, if possible, even madder than the scowling locals. The captain couldn't seem to understand what had happened, even though Nick had explained it twice. This might top all the awards for Most Embarrassing Event of My Life, Nick was thinking.

"Tell me once more how you jumped on the wrong fucking truck?" Oliver was shouting at the other end of the world. Nick could hear him slugging down milk straight from a carton for his ulcer.

On the other side of the desk, Charlie was going through mug shots, thousands of square-faced, almond-eyed men with straight black hair. "Christ," he was mumbling to himself, "these mutts are . . . definitely not him, there's another definite . . . well, maybe . . . definitely a maybe . . . oh, Christ . . ."

Captain Oliver was quieter now. The milk must have helped. His voice came deliberately and almost sadly across the thousands of miles. "Remember my office?" he said. "A desk and a chair. Only now it's just a mountain of shit."

"I didn't know what names to expect. The guy said

Inspector Nashida, so I figured he was it. I had no way of verifying I.D.'s, no—"

"Don't give me goddamned excuses. I want to know how it happened. Run it by me in slow motion, just once more."

Nick sighed and told the story again.

"Nine definite maybes," Charlie muttered, jotting another I.D. number down and shutting the first of many thick albums. He opened the next book, scrutinized the first shot, held it up for Nick to see. As he talked into the phone, Nick looked over at the photo and shrugged. Maybe.

An elderly woman, stooped and carrying a heavy box from which wisps of steam trailed pungent scents, made her way through the big room, stopping at each desk to open the lid of her carrier. She reached deep inside and handed out neatly wrapped boxes of food to the men who signaled her from their desks. When she arrived at the desk next to the one Nick and Charlie were using, she spoke to the plainclothes paper-pusher. As she reached in to serve him his lunch, she pointed to Nick and Charlie and asked him a string of run-together questions, obviously about them and what they were doing on her turf.

The guy at the next desk was apparently their contact—at any rate he had been put in charge of them until they could see a higher-up. He had not tried to speak to them but had indicated with gestures that they were to sit at that desk and wait.

Whatever the guy said in answer to the old woman's question made her laugh, and she covered her toothless mouth with one hand. Charlie looked up. He was sure she had asked if they were foreign criminals and when the desk jockey said that, no, they were cops, she had thought it was hilarious. She stole a shy look at handsome Charlie. He smiled back. The old lady set down a bowl of steaming noodles at the desk jockey's elbow and he paid her.

She bowed and picked up her heavy burden, scurrying past Nick and Charlie with quick little steps.

"Hey," Charlie called, "who's in charge of the coffee?"

"I went by the book," Nick was explaining over again to Oliver. "If they were legit the I.D.'s would have been the same, wouldn't they? The paperwork was in Jap, for Christ's sake—"

The man at the next desk was eating his noodles, with the bowl held close to his mouth, shoveling it in with chopsticks. He made loud slurping noises, which Charlie had read was the polite thing to do. That must have been true, because from all around them came the same slurping noises. The delicious smell and the gusty sounds were making Charlie salivate. He pulled out the phrase book and found what he wanted to say.

"Su-mi-ma-san. Noodles." The man at the next desk didn't look up or slow down the avid enjoyment of his lunch. "Where can I score a cup of coffee?" Charlie asked in something close to desperation.

His only contact looked at him, smiled politely, set the empty bowl aside, and returned to his work. He had a *hanko* in his hand—a small cylinder of highly polished wood which held an intricate one-of-a-kind set of characters engraved in its base. The man, who was middle-aged and had a look of intelligent resignation on his nearly unlined face, sat before two tall stacks of papers, taking one sheet at a time and stamping it with his *hanko,* placing it neatly in his "out" box. He did it mechanically, over and over and over and over again, with no sign of boredom or weariness or interest. He worked with the efficiency and passion of a machine.

"Unbelievable," Charlie said. "These people are buying up Fifth Avenue, but try to get a cup of coffee and all they can do is smile."

On the phone, Oliver was asking Nick, "Have you spoken to anyone in charge yet?"

"Not yet," Nick said. "I'm working on it." He looked over at a desk at the end of the room, where a male secretary sat facing the rows of bullpen workers. Catching his eye, Nick held up his wrist and pointed to the face of his watch. The secretary smiled and held up one finger.

Covering the mouthpiece of the phone, Nick muttered to Charlie, "The next time he does that, I'm gonna cut it off, I swear to God."

"Wrong finger, pal," Charlie said.

"What? What? What'd you say?" Oliver shouted on the other end of the phone.

"Nothing, Cap. The major cheese here's going to see us in exactly one minute," Nick told him.

Charlie slid one of the books of mug shots around on the desk so Nick could scan a random page: a sheet of men who could be brothers. Nick looked at it and cupped his hand over the phone again. "Un-fucking-canny," he commented. "Identical strangers."

"Captain," he said into the phone, "I'm going to salvage this situation."

"Nick, worry about salvaging your ass," the captain told him. "You just put yourself in the toilet and pulled the handle."

"What the hell is that supposed to mean?" Nick groaned.

"Who are we kidding, man?" Charlie muttered. In desperation he pulled the album back and held it up for the man at the next desk, still slurping his noodles, to see. *"Dozo,* boss," he said. "You got anything else for us besides your kamikaze yearbook here?"

Down at the end of the room, the secretary's phone rang. Everyone in the room looked up, waiting. The secretary picked up the receiver, listened, and nodded, bowing reflexively to the unseen caller. *"Hai,"* he said over and over. *"Hai. Hai."* He hung up and gestured to Nick and Charlie's man. Everyone else in the neat rows of desks went back to their work. The stocky man, who was unusually tall for a Japanese, sprang up, grabbed his suit jacket from the back of his chair and put it on.

"Banzai," Charlie muttered.

"There are some people who think it's convenient that the one prisoner you lost in your whole life looked like he could afford it." Oliver had lowered his voice and he sounded more sad than mad, but Nick was stung. If even his own captain thought maybe he took money from Sato to let him slip, his rep was in a lot worse condition than he had realized. Getting Sato meant more than Sato's neck; his own was on the blade now too.

But he barked into the phone as if the accusation had bounced off without a dent. "Those bastards can kiss my ass," he told Oliver loudly. "Until he's delivered he's still mine."

Charlie looked up at the new anger in Nick's voice. "What?" he mouthed.

Their man with the noodles was now standing at their desk almost at attention, waiting. They looked up at him and waited too. The man gestured toward the secretary's desk and the imposing office door behind it.

"Gotta go, Captain," Nick shouted into the phone, and hung up. "Action," he muttered. "Fabulous!"

He and Charlie got up. The middle-aged functionary walked briskly between them down the narrow aisle.

"I'm gonna tell this character, in detail, how much I liked being kept waiting," Nick said to Charlie.

"Remember," Charlie warned him, "it's his jungle."

They talked as if they were alone—well, for all practical purposes they felt that way. None of the men sitting at rows of identical desks in identical suits or uniforms looked up as they passed.

"I'll make nice," Nick said. By way of illustration, he smiled at their guide, who caught it immediately and smiled back.

"I just hope they got one noodle-slurping Nip in this building who speaks fucking English," Nick told Charlie loudly.

They rounded the secretary's desk and stopped at the office door. Their escort knocked once. There was a muffled response from inside. Their guide snapped to attention and reached into his suit-jacket pocket. He brought out a small business card—engraved—and presented it to Nick with a quiet flourish.

"Assistant Inspector Matsumoto Masahiro," he said with a very, very slight hint of a bow. "Criminal-investigation station, Osaka Prefectural Police, and I do speak fucking English."

Nick looked at Charlie, Charlie looked at Nick—both were uncharacteristically speechless for a moment. They both looked at their guide, but there was absolutely nothing in Masahiro's expression to indicate how much he surely must have been enjoying this moment.

"Another lousy sneak attack," Nick managed to mutter under his breath, but loud enough for Masahiro to hear, as the assistant inspector opened the door politely for them.

"Gentlemen," he said without cracking a smile, stepping aside to let them precede him into the room.

The man standing behind the desk, extending his hand to them, was clearly the major brass. There were two other men in the room, one in police uniform.

"May I introduce Detective Sergeant Nicholas Conklin," Masahiro said formally, "and Detective Charlie Vincent." He then repeated it in Japanese—they barely recognized their own names when translated.

"And may I present Chief Superintendent Ohashi, Inspector Inoue, and Inspector Kinoshita," he finished.

The Japanese men bowed slightly. Nick shook Ohashi's extended hand and then Charlie did, and then the Japanese men bowed. Charlie bowed in return but Nick did not. They shook the hands of the other two officers and finally, Nick thought, they could get down to business.

But first, they ordered tea.

8

One hour later, after tea had been elaborately made in front of them and finally served, with compliments all around, translated by Masahiro, the room was filled with cigarette smoke and Nick Conklin was filled with frustration to a level he had seldom, if ever, tolerated. Matsumoto Masahiro almost felt sympathy for him. The American in his slouchy clothing and disrespectful ways was simply the creature of another culture; it was probably not his fault that he was feeling too impatient to observe the rules of professional etiquette.

When the first cups of tea had been drunk and a second round prepared, the American again spoke of his most urgent concern. Now the time was right to circle around to the business at hand, and this time, Ohashi would not change the subject.

"Can we begin now?" Nick Conklin asked.

Masahiro nodded politely. The second American, called Charlie (very hard to pronounce), sighed with audible relief. Perhaps he feared his superior was about to commit some outrageous act? But now Conklin spoke quietly. "Okay, then. Could you please ask the superintendent if his people have any witnesses from the airport?"

Masahiro translated this into Japanese for the superintendent: "He wishes to know if we have any witnesses."

The three officers who were in Ohashi's office when Masahiro and the Americans had come in had said nothing throughout the hour, but sat sipping their tea, politely appearing not to listen or understand until it was their turn to be addressed directly.

Ohashi listened thoughtfully and then said, in a most genial tone of voice (Masahiro thought), "It's none of his business."

Masahiro's face remained impassive. The American detective was studying him curiously but would find nothing to read there. "The superintendent says it is possible," he translated.

This diplomatic answer did not satisfy Nick Conklin. "Possible?" he ranted. "Manned space flight is possible."

Masahiro was puzzled by this; it made no sense to him. "Manned . . . space flight?" he repeated.

The second American chimed in, to explain the erratic words of his superior. "He's really zoned out from all the flying," he told Masahiro. "Jet lag—you know."

Conklin looked at Charlie Vincent in a way that was not complimentary. Charlie Vincent shrugged his shoulders. Masahiro understood. The younger man was trying, in his peculiarly Western way, to be tactful. Masahiro nodded and translated for his superintendent.

"He's tired from jet lag," he told Ohashi.

The secretary ceremoniously lifted the finely painted teapot and began to pour fresh tea into the cups of the guests. But Detective Sergeant Conklin quickly placed his hand over his cup—apparently his way of indicating that he did not care to participate further in the tea ritual. The secretary, slow to comprehend such a strange and rude gesture, did not stop in time to prevent the pouring of hot tea, which now ran over the back of Conklin's hand.

The secretary was horribly embarrassed and did not know how to redeem the situation. He bowed and wiped the table and Conklin's hand and even the lap of the American's blue jeans where the tea had run down, but Conklin brushed him away with no thought for the secretary's terrible loss of face.

"I said no tea, thank you! May I please have some coffee?" The secretary backed away, mumbling apologies and finally scurrying for the door. Masahiro spoke quickly to his retreating back, translating the American's request and creating an apology for him.

"Look," Conklin said, "we're wasting valuable time. If you'd tell me who Sato is, why the meeting in New York, what it was that changed hands, maybe I could crack the airport thing."

Masahiro translated, very fast. He sensed the growing impatience of his superior to the brutish attitude and demands of the Americans.

"I want you to translate *every word I say,*" Conklin told him. "Understand?"

"Yes, I understand," Masahiro said calmly.

Superintendent Ohashi spoke his true feelings in level and unrevealing tones. "Look at these two slobs," he told Masahiro scornfully. "Made in America. Tell him he doesn't have to drink our tea. But he should apologize. This whole situation is due to his negligence. I use a polite word for it."

Masahiro nodded, and translated for Nick Conklin: "Through your negligence, a man we sought for a long time has been lost. You do not have to drink tea, but you should apologize."

Conklin exploded. Masahiro knew that apparent loss of self-control such as shouting and becoming flushed in the face was perfectly acceptable behavior in a professional business encounter among Westerners, but he couldn't help thinking that the American was going too far. The conversation was instantly heated and hard to follow—much less interpret—in two languages simultaneously, but Masahiro tried.

"Our negligence?" Conklin stormed. "Who let people carrying your documents, wearing your uniforms, waltz through a secure area? We'll take our share of the heat, but no way we're taking the rap for this!"

"No, it was not our negligence, they had documents and uniforms . . ." Masahiro interpreted.

Conklin took the document he had received from the phoney cop out of his pocket and dropped it on the table.

"Bite," he said slowly. "Fall. Heat."

Masahiro translated.

"Blame," Charlie Vincent chimed in.

"Don't blame it on us," Masahiro translated.

Superintendent Ohashi leaned across the tea table and picked up the document between his thumb and middle finger. He took a cursory glance at it and snorted. "This document is an insurance policy," he said in slow, heavily accented English.

Nick and Charlie were still recovering from the shock of hearing him speak the language, and wondering if everybody in this country was bilingual except them, when Ohashi went on—in English, broken but clearly understandable.

"The police will find *your* escaped prisoner," he assured them calmly.

"We *are* the police," the younger American responded.

The superintendent shook his head. "You are foreigners," he told them. "Nothing more than observers —interested observers. Go home, Detective."

He had dismissed them. He got up from the tea table, walked across the office to his desk and sat behind it. Nick followed him, planting his hands firmly on the desk and leaning over in a most rude way to confront the superintendent directly in his face. Properly, Ohashi stared past the foreigner as if he were not doing that.

"I'm an uptown minute from throwing you people an international incident that will make your heads swim," Detective Nick Conklin told Superintendent Ohashi firmly. "Until someone signs for him, his ass is mine. So either we cooperate on this or I'm going to the newspapers, the embassy, Jesus Christ on the Cross, your Emperor, and the goddamned Bluebird of Happiness if I have to!"

When the outburst subsided, Ohashi, still ignoring the provocation of the American's face in his, spoke to the men who had taken up their places flanking his desk. "It may be useful to keep them for a few days," he said thoughtfully in their own language.

"Hai," agreed the plainclothesman.

"We'll keep them on a leash, then send them back when we're done. Tell them we're on our way downstairs."

"Yes, yes, sir," the officer said. He saluted the superintendent, turned smartly on his heel, and left the office.

Nick Conklin continued to lean forward on the desk of the superintendent, but still Ohashi showed better manners and was able to ignore him. Standing, the superintendent walked around his desk. Before reaching the door, he turned and spoke again, in English, to the bewildered Americans.

"All right, you may stay, gentlemen," he said. "Please just leave your guns."

"What are you talking about?" Nick Conklin asked, showing all his emotions in his sharply featured face. "We're cops!"

"Here you are civilians. It is illegal for you to carry guns," Ohashi explained patiently.

The American detective shook his head angrily and seemed about to erupt again. It was astonishing to Masahiro how much energy was expended with all this show of feelings—how did they ever get anything done?

The second American, Charlie, also saw the incipient explosion, and spoke softly. "Boss," he said to Conklin. And to Superintendent Ohashi, he said, "We understand."

Nick Conklin hesitated only a minute, and then he unholstered his .38 and put it on the desk in front of him. Charlie Vincent put his own gun on the table as well. At that, one of the uniformed police opened the office door to allow the guests to depart.

Superintendent Ohashi was at the door. "Excuse me," he said. "All your guns, gentlemen, if you please."

Conklin reached inside his jacket and around to his back, where he unloosed another gun from a belt holster. The young cop did the same with his backup, which was on his ankle.

Ohashi made a small businesslike bow. "We will appreciate your coming with us now, please." He stood at the door and waited for them to precede him.

"All right," Conklin said, "but we need someone who will help us out."

Masahiro understood that the Americans intended to pursue Sato on their own. He thought them very foolish for this, but yet he understood. Back in the long-ago days when he was on active duty, he surely would have done the same. Not that he would ever have lost a prisoner in such an infamous, stupid way, in a foreign country where he did not speak the language or understand the customs . . .

"Of course, Detective," Ohashi was saying. "You shall have one of our top officers."

He turned to Masahiro and spoke again in Japanese to him. "Don't let them out of your sight. Report to me every comment, every action, every reaction."

Masahiro was stunned. He had been sitting behind a desk for many years now, waiting out his retirement, which was not far off. Now he was to begin again, on the streets, in charge of these two erratic and impulsive Americans in their bizarre determination to go where they were not familiar, locate what they could not see, interfere with the lawful and proper work of the respected Osaka Prefecture.

"*Hai,*" Masahiro responded automatically, with a bow to his superior.

Ohashi left the room, with the other officers. Masahiro was alone in the room with the Americans.

He permitted himself a low groan. "*Ai-ta-ta,*" he almost whispered under his breath. It was almost a sort of prayer for guidance, as well as a small complaint.

"Okay," Conklin said. "Where's our cop? We pick him up downstairs or what? Let's get going."

Masahiro smiled and bowed formally. "It is my honor," he said.

He wondered fleetingly, as he led the way out, why the gods of retirement had seen fit to fuck up his peaceful last years on the force.

9

Masahiro grabbed a worn, seedy briefcase and led them down to a clerk's office, where he requisitioned a car and driver. He rode shotgun, with Nick and Charlie in the back seat. The siren wailed as they cruised the crowded, colorful streets of Osaka at night. Charlie held his guidebook in his hand, flipping through the pages and referring to photos of temples and busy squares as they passed by.

"'Osaka is Japan's number-two city in population and number-one city in industry,'" he read out loud. "'It is called the Venice of Japan'—hey, how about that—'because of the many canals they once had, but of which few remain because of the city's modernization.'" He looked up from the book out at the bustling whirl of vividly lit bars, nightclubs, restaurants, shops, and throngs of people in the streets.

Nick stared alternately at the back of Masahiro's head or out the window, as every now and then Masahiro spoke up loudly, pointing straight ahead at his idea of interesting tourist attractions. "That is called a *koban,* that police box. There are six hundred *kobans* to serve the people of Osaka," he said.

"What was that business with Oliver all about?" Charlie asked Nick quietly.

"Shit rolling downhill."

"Huh?"

"This is the *Dotonburi,"* Masahiro said, with a sweeping gesture covering the neon-lit avenue they turned onto. "Here is the center for hostess bars, restaurants, it is the so-called pleasure district, one might say. Perhaps like your own Square Times."

"Times Square," Charlie corrected him. He craned his neck to take it all in. Times Square was never so brightly lit, so chaotic in its garish clash of jammed-together doorways, each with its shill, crowds of people laughing and drunk, clashing music amplified a thousand times over a thousand different systems, blasted out onto the street where cars inched erratically through the heedless revelers. "But," added Masahiro, "no crime here."

"No crime, now that's really something," Nick said. "It's amazing. So—you think you could tell us how come your people were so hot to get Sato back here?"

"Yes, please," said their keeper agreeably. And that was all he said. He continued to look straight ahead as their driver managed to wend through the throngs without actually killing anyone.

A look of pure exasperation passed between Nick and Charlie in the back seat. A slashing glare of red cut across Nick's face, reflected from the huge letters of a neon sign. This guy's a real winner, Charlie's look said. Yeah, we got a time-serving desk jockey helping us along—some joke, Nick's eyes flashed back.

Somewhere in this crowded city, or anywhere in this totally alien country, Sato was enjoying his freedom and getting farther away by the second. And what were they doing to find him? They were getting a guided tour of the Venice of Japan, where the picturesque canals had all been paved over. Masahiro was talking with the driver, apparently discussing where to make the next turn.

"Hey, Chief," Nick snapped. "I asked you a question."

Masahiro settled the directions with the driver and then half-turned in his seat to look back at his passengers. He was not smiling, but his expression was always pleasant, alert, and he seemed to have no problem with who was in control here. He was.

"Ah, the man *you* lost was suspected of murder. Perhaps it is not much in your prefecture, but it is very unusual here. I've heard you have more murders in New York prefecture in a week than we have in our city in a year, Detective Conklin. Is that statistic accurate?"

Nick groaned. "Spare us the *National Geographic,* and tell me about the case, Matsumoto. Like about the victim, for starters. Who is this Sato suspected of killing?"

"Assistant Inspector Matsumoto Masahiro," his mentor corrected him stiffly.

Nick pointed a thumb at his own chest. "I'm

Conklin," he said. He jerked his thumb toward Charlie. "This is Vincent. Listen, Masahiro, we don't have time for spit and polish, okay? So—who was the victim?"

"I would refer you to our files for details, but he was a Damascene maker."

The car had finally worked its way out of the carnival atmosphere and turned onto a wide boulevard lined with huge department stores and shops whose windows were all filled with mannequins in trendy fashions. Here, too, everything was lit brightly, although there were fewer people and a more sedate atmosphere.

"A Damascene maker," Nick repeated, trying to make any sense out of that. The deeper they got into this, the more hopeless it seemed that they would ever understand a goddamned thing. He looked glumly out of his window at the signs that said nothing to him. How could you even tell what street you were on, what district you were in? How could you find a Most Wanted who didn't want to be found?

"Yeah, we have the same problem in New York," Charlie was telling Masahiro. "Our Damascene makers are dropping like flies."

Masahiro pointed ahead. "Ah, here is another one of our six hundred *kobans*."

Nick sighed. "Tell us, Assistant Inspector, when you're not doing the Chamber of Commerce tour, what do you do for a living?"

Without turning around, Masahiro explained, "I update files for the National Police. Compile statistics and coordinate. Thirty-three years I've served our department. It's been my honor."

"Pencil jockey," Charlie murmured automatically.

"Shine," Nick said at the same instant.

Masahiro turned, smiling. "Beg pardon?" he asked.

"That's what we call you in New York," Charlie explained. "Terms of great honor."

It was impossible to know whether Masahiro understood or not, but Nick and Charlie were up to here with it by now and beginning to suspect they had been made the butts of a scheme to keep them impotent and out of the way.

As the car approached a major intersection, some calls came in over the radio, and Masahiro picked up the mike to ask a couple of terse questions. Nick thought he heard him say Ohashi's name, but he wasn't sure. Masahiro finished the call-in and spoke quickly to the driver, pointing. They turned onto one of the brightly lit streets that fanned out from the square. There seemed to be mostly nightclubs and restaurants, but here they were not piled on top of each other and the atmosphere was much less frenetic than back in the "pleasure district."

The car sped up, swerved around a couple of corners, sirens shrieking, and came to a stop in front of an awning. There were two giant neon signs, one in Japanese characters and the other in English: CLUB MIYAKO. Something was definitely happening here. A major-size crowd was gathered in front of the club, and several police cars were there before them, pulled up to the door.

Masahiro climbed out of the car. He looked back through the open window at Nick and Charlie, addressing his words to Nick. "Stay close, please, Detective Conklin."

They scrambled out. Nick met Charlie's eyes and he muttered an old catchphrase in the language that partners develop between themselves over a period of time. "Asses and elbows, Charlie." Charlie understood. At the quizzical look this got from their leader, Nick muttered, "Cook your calculator, Matsumoto." But—probably fortunately—the assistant inspector made no sign that he had heard. He strode through the crowd, which opened a respectful aisle for him. Nick and Charlie had to hurry to keep up.

Inside the club, everything was at a standstill. Thick smoke clouded the already dim air. There was no music, only the sound of many voices ranging from nervous to strident. A host of police officers were separating patrons and employees, interviewing them and taking down information.

Masahiro made his way through the bar and across the dance floor, weaving around the crowds of tiny tables where half-eaten dinners, cocktails, bottles of *sake* and beer had been abandoned. Nick and Charlie followed closely as Masahiro pushed through a pair of swinging doors, and they found themselves in the kitchen of the club. It was suffocatingly hot and surprisingly small in comparison to the large patron area.

Superintendent Ohashi was there, supervising. A man lay dead on the floor, his head propped up against the wall in a corner. There was a lot of blood. Kneeling beside the corpse, a white-gloved officer reached into the dead man's throat with forceps and came up with a hundred-dollar bill, American. He held it up for Ohashi to see and then stashed it in a plastic bag held open for him by another cop with another pair of white gloves.

"Think he's got two fives for a ten?" Charlie quipped.

Masahiro, standing aside, waved Nick and Charlie to move in. Nick knelt by the body and took a good look. Carefully, he picked up the wrist with two fingers and turned it over. The wrist turned easily.

"No defense wounds," Nick said. "Nice, clean, right-handed cut down from . . ." He pointed to the man's throat. "There."

Charlie was kneeling, too, and now he touched the man's chest with the back of his hand. "The perp left wet," he told Nick. "Body heat hasn't caught up with the room. He's fresh."

Nick was staring at the face of the corpse. "From the airport," he said after a moment. "One of the phoney cops."

"You're certain?" Masahiro spoke quickly, stepping forward.

Nick nodded and stood up. Masahiro began conferring with Ohashi in rapid Japanese. Finally he looked back at Nick and Charlie and gave them a short bow. "That's all," he told them. "The superintendent thanks you very much."

"Okay," said Nick. He felt a whole lot better about the tack things were taking now. So Ohashi hadn't dismissed them with a babysitter to keep them off his back after all.

What was it Masahiro had been saying about the statistics on murders in this town? Looks like the odds just went down. But he wouldn't rub it in. Let's just find that fucker, he thought to himself. Come on, let's get on with it. Who is this stiff, and where'd he hang out, and who were his buddies, and what's the connection to Sato?

Masahiro was politely pointing toward the kitchen door. "Please," he said, clearly indicating that Nick and Charlie were expected to leave quietly.

"Whoa, whoa," Nick told him. "Fill me in. What you got here? Did Sato do his own guy?"

"Please don't interfere," Masahiro told him firmly. "I've been ordered to take you to your hotel."

Nick called over to Ohashi. "Hey, what am I, chopped liver? This is my job. I'm in on this."

"You are observers," Masahiro said.

Nick looked like he was about to explode. Charlie stopped him. "We'll get more from a quiet look around than from a fight, boss."

Nick glared at Ohashi. "Usually someone kisses you when you get fucked." He shot a glance at Masahiro. "Translate," Nick said shortly. Then he strode out of the kitchen. Charlie and Masahiro followed him. Masahiro had not translated; perhaps it had not been necessary.

As they headed down the narrow hallway toward the main room, they passed a door that stood ajar. Showing a bit of natural curiosity, the detectives glanced inside as they passed. They were brought up short and stood staring for a stunned minute. The room was lined with mirrors.

A delicately beautiful, slender, but full-bodied young Japanese hostess was kneeling on the carpeted floor. Police officers were talking to her, asking questions. She was dressed in a clinging gown completely covered with shimmering black and white sequins that flashed in the light and reflected millions of sparkles back from all the mirrors. There was something else reflected, too—bright red blood, dripping from the woman's forearms and hands.

Abruptly, the door was shut in their faces. Nick and Charlie hurried to catch up with Masahiro.

10

*I*n the main room of the Club Miyako, the uniformed police were creating some order out of chaos.
Some customers and employees were being taken, one
by one, into a side room for questioning; others were
herded into groups on either side of the club to wait.
Someone had thought to turn overhead work lights
on, and the eerie business of conducting a murder
enquiry under soft diffused blue was partly alleviated.
Masahiro headed through the room with Charlie right
behind him, but Nick suddenly fell back.

Something blond had caught his eye. In a large back
room that was a kind of private annex to the main
lounge, he saw a whole bevy of young hostesses
twittering and hovering like anxious little humming-
birds around a tall, knockout blue-eyed blonde. It
sounded like she was consoling the girls in their own

lingo and it looked like she was dabbing with a handkerchief at bloodstains on her nice white silk dress.

Nick moved in closer but the ladies seemed too preoccupied to notice him. He got right up to the blonde and squatted down alongside her. He took a minute to admire her upswept curls and expensive pearl earrings, the sweep of her soft white throat and the way her body enhanced the white silk dress she was wearing. When she finished speaking the hostesses seemed to be quieted down somewhat; clearly they respected her and she was their leader—maybe "madam" would be a more specific word, but he wasn't going to assume anything; not yet. She stared at him, waiting for him to say what the hell he was doing there.

"You want to try a little peroxide?" he asked her with his most innocent and charming smile.

The blonde took a good long minute to size him up. She was really a beauty, not exactly a teenager anymore but then neither was he, and he never had liked teenagers even when he was one. This lady had big blue eyes that looked right at you and waited for you to state your business.

"For the bloodstains," he said. "It always works for me."

"Who are you? What are you?" she asked. The sound of English seemed to have a quieting effect on the other ladies; they stood watching in a kind of semiprotective circle around her. Judging by her accent, or lack of one, Nick would have guessed culture, education—Boston, maybe.

He dug for his wallet and flipped his badge for her. "Detective Sergeant Nick Conklin," he said.

He put the badge away. "Where'd the blood come from?"

One of the hostesses bent down and said something in the blonde's ear. Whatever it was made the others giggle. They covered their mouths with their hands.

The blonde laughed too, and translated: "She wants to know if you're the fool who lost Sato at the airport."

Nick didn't answer. Partly he didn't know what to say and partly he was too pissed off and partly he had the weird feeling that he ought to cover his mouth with his hand, too. He just stood there like a jerk.

"Just off the plane and you make the evening news," said the blonde. "Nice work."

The hostesses went off into hilarious fits again.

"Maybe I should stick around and run for congress," Nick said.

The blonde had a nice smile, human and warm, even teeth, and probably a nice even temperament. He got that feeling, anyhow. What she said was, "Americans who are less than perfect please them."

On the other side of the big room, Charlie was trying to keep Masahiro from being nervous about letting Nick loose. He tried everything he could think of to detain him, to keep the assistant inspector from hauling Nick away from the annex and all the goodies he had found there.

"Some joint," Charlie said, looking everywhere but in the direction of the annex. The furnishings were elegant and lavish, from the thick smooth carpets to the silk-upholstered chairs and gold-painted ceilings. "Are you known here?"

"Me?" Masahiro said, and he almost cracked a

smile. His black hair was combed straight down on his brow, with only the slightest tinges of gray in it. Charlie never would have guessed that he was near retirement age. Maybe people just stayed younger longer in this country—or maybe the desk cop never had any stress to put lines in his face and snow on his head. "I could never afford to come to a place like this," Masahiro told him.

Stalling, giving Nick as much time as he could, Charlie put on an air of friendly disbelief, babbling whatever came into his head. "The money you people make over here?" he scoffed. "Hey, this is Japan! Millionaire cops. We've heard all about you guys. You can skip the modesty, fella."

A beautiful young woman in an elaborately embroidered blue silk kimono hurried past them. "Umm," Charlie said. "Very fine." Masahiro started toward the annex. Charlie touched the arm of his suit jacket. "Look," he said, nodding at the hostess, "since I'm new in town and you want to make a nice impression, why don't you introduce me?"

Masahiro looked at him incredulously. "But I told you. I could not know her."

"Show her the tin, Masa. The badge. You and me, we'll question her closely."

"Do you think she's done something?" Masahiro asked him.

Charlie grinned. "Maybe. I'll tell you what—give me fifteen minutes and some translating and I guarantee she will!"

Masahiro shook his head, almost sadly. "You make jokes on me?"

"No, man, honest, that's just something we do back

home if we want to get to know someone, it's harm-less, and it damn near always works. You don't pull shit like that here, huh?"

Masahiro shook his head again. He started edging toward the annex again. Nick could be seen in earnest conversation with the blonde now.

Charlie linked his arm through the assistant inspec-tor's. "Well, you know what, Masa—you and I have got to do some real cultural exchanging here, now. We could learn a lot about each other's ways, you know, and maybe it would help us work together, understand each other's methods and such."

Out of the corner of his eye, Nick was relieved to see Charlie and Masahiro move back against the far wall of the main room. He was still in their sights but somehow Charlie had managed to cool out the assist-ant inspector, for the moment, anyway.

"You still haven't told me about the blood," he said to the blonde.

She looked at him coolly, trying to decide whether she needed to cooperate with this guy or not. Some-thing in his nice American eyes told her, probably wrongly, to trust him. Well, she'd go just so far. "The girl who found the body was upset. I put my arms around her. Wouldn't you?" she answered.

He didn't have much time. He used the shoot-questions-fast-and-from-all-directions technique.

"You from Boston?"

"Chicago," she said.

"Where'd you learn to speak Japanese?"

She smiled, just a little. "Chicago."

It made him smile, too. "What do they call you back in Chicago?"

She withdrew the smile. "Same thing they call me here. Joyce."

"Nice. Did you know the victim, Joyce?"

She shook her head. The color was absolutely authentic, he would have sworn it. "A couple of guys met for drinks," she said. "This is how it turned out, that's all I know."

"Did you see the killer leave?" Nick pressed her.

"Yeah, sure. And he wrote down his name and address and asked me to give it to you. Anything else?"

"Yeah," Nick said. "Why the bullshit?"

She looked him straight in the eyes and told the straight truth. "Because you could get me killed, Detective," she said. "There's a war going on and these people don't take prisoners."

She looked so deeply sad for an instant Nick had this crazy idea that he'd like to put his arms around her. But this was leading somewhere. He felt the excitement starting in his gut that meant he was on to something, at last. Carefully, persuasively (he hoped), he asked her, "What are you talking about, Joyce?"

She seemed to be amazed that he didn't already know. Clearly, she wasn't telling him any big secret: "Big gang war. Between Sato and an old-time boss. A guy named Sugai," she said flatly. "You're chasing Sato, and you don't know that much?"

A uniform came over to them, and indicated to Joyce that it was her turn to go into the interrogation room. He waited to escort her.

"How many people know about this?" Nick asked quickly.

Joyce turned to go with the cop. She had a little,

almost wistful, smile on her beautiful lips as she told Nick, over her shoulder, "Counting you and me? About eleven million."

She headed for the room that had been set aside for questioning, leaving Nick feeling just a little bit like a slow-witted kid in school. He strode across the main room to rejoin Charlie and Masahiro.

"Did you learn anything from that woman, Detective Conklin?" Masahiro asked as they left the club. Thick crowds of sensation-seekers, no different anywhere in the world, still clotted the sidewalk and street in front of the club.

"Why would she tell me anything?" Nick retorted. "I'm just an observer." They moved through the crowd to the waiting car and driver. "Tell Ohashi I'll report to him when he reports to me," Nick said. He stepped up to the car and banged with his fist on the trunk. The driver snapped the lock from inside the car and the trunk swung open.

"We both have our orders," Masahiro said reasonably. "I'm a police officer just like you, Detective."

"Wrong," Nick told him. "You're a suit-and-tie. You can tell your boss that one good hand job deserves another."

"I don't understand," said Masahiro. He and Nick, almost the same height and build, faced each other under the streetlight. For once, the assistant inspector let some concern flicker across his pleasant, impassive face.

Nick reached into the trunk of the car and lifted out his small overnight bag and Charlie's much larger garment bag.

Charlie watched in surprise. "Somebody do something to somebody?" he asked Nick.

"Get out your Greyhound Tour map and get directions to our hotel," Nick told him. He slammed the trunk down and shouldered the bags.

"Huh? But Nick—"

"Just do it."

Charlie pulled out the map of Osaka and went around to the driver's window. A routine followed which might have drawn a lot of laughs if a professional mime did it on a talk show, but at two in the morning on a side street in a major city whose map was spelled out in letters looking more like *sukiyaki* than an alphabet, getting directions in a language you couldn't savvy was not amusing.

"You do not wish to ride?" Masahiro asked, astonished and, perhaps, dismayed.

"We'll walk," said Nick. "What I want from you is information. Sato's file, the paperwork from tonight, and anything else relevant to this case. I want it and I want it translated into English. By oh-nine-hundred tomorrow, A.M. Got it, Matsumoto?"

Charlie came around from his dumb-show dialogue with the driver and Nick handed him the garment bag. "Let's go," he said.

"Sure, Nick," Charlie said, but he was damned confused. Personally, he had nothing against Masahiro and figured they could work together. But Nick always—almost always—knew what he was doing, and Charlie was his partner and his pal and his junior and so what the hell. He bowed to Masahiro. *"Kon-bonwa,* Chief," he told him.

Masahiro bowed in return. Then he stood erect and looked at Nick. "Very well," he said. "You will have a long walk to your hotel."

Nick turned to go. "Don't worry," he said over his shoulder. "If we get lost we'll ask a cop."

Masahiro stood watching them until they were out of sight, the hotheaded, inscrutable Americans, carrying their baggage and striding off in the wrong direction for the place they wished to go.

11

*A*t two on a weekday morning the streets of Osaka were still crowded with late revelers, clusters of businessmen and clerks out celebrating with loud laughter and drunken shouts. Nick and Charlie stood out like the aliens they were, feeling more outlandish every minute—too tall, too light-haired, too sober, and very, very lost.

They walked the way they thought they had come, and as they walked, they filled each other in. Nick told Charlie what he had learned from Joyce.

"I can't believe Noodles didn't tell us a damn thing about any of that," Charlie said. "And I was almost getting to where I could tolerate him. Maybe we should turn here, does that look familiar?"

"Suits are suits," Nick told his partner. "He's a rubber-stamp mechanic. No guts, no brains. If he had to face a mutt with a butter knife he'd shit in his pants. Ohashi assigned him to us for a big joke."

They turned up a street that looked like all the other streets. Neon lights and all-night noodle parlors. But it was slower now; even the bars were beginning to shut down, and there were fewer people than before. They seemed to be heading determinedly for their homes now.

"I think that's the corner where the hotel is, down at the end of the block," Charlie said. He was wishing he hadn't packed so many clothes. He shifted the bulging garment bag from one shoulder to the other.

By the time they reached the corner the streets were almost deserted. It was after three A.M. The wind jiggled the paper lanterns hanging outside the shuttered stores. Only an occasional cluster of salarymen hurrying home so they could get up and get to the office again.

"Just around the corner." Nick groaned. "Isn't that what your guidebook said our hotel was? Right off the main drag? Wasn't that the fucking main drag?"

"Whoa, wait a minute, buster. Who was it said 'we'll walk'? Why, I do believe it was Nick Conklin, that well-known fresh-air-and-exercise fanatic."

"You were supposed to get directions," Nick said.

"I was supposed to get—unbelievable!" Charlie sputtered. "Unbelievable, man! Do I look like I work at the U.N.? It was in Jap!"

Nick set his bag down on the deserted sidewalk. The frantic city noises had quieted to an almost eerie silence. Except for an occasional car—but never an empty taxi—only the wind and their own voices echoed in the streets. "Let me see the map," he told Charlie.

Charlie unloaded his bag and shook his head. "No, forget the map. Forget the fucking map. It's in Jap too, and since we don't know where we are, we couldn't exactly figure out which way is even up on the map." He looked up at the intersection signs, with arrows pointing and clearly lettered characters delineating the streets—in Kanji. "All I know is the Bronx is up and the Battery's down," Charlie said. "What's your next great idea? Swim to New York?"

"I wonder what time it is in New York," Nick said.

"I wonder what day it is. When's the last time we had any sleep? Tuesday? Wednesday? What day is it here? Where are we?" Charlie shut up and waited for Nick to come up with something.

"Ask someone," Nick said.

Charlie sat down on the curb. "Again? Maybe this time I'll try *'hola, señor. Donde esta la Hotel Meiji?'* How's that sound? What the hell, it might work."

There were a couple of suits coming their way, but they put their dark heads down and hurried past the foreign devils.

Suddenly serious, Charlie said, "Nicky, you know this isn't our jungle. Maybe we should cut our losses and let the locals handle it."

"I can't do that, Charlie. Some people back home think I got rich on the flight over here."

"What?" Charlie was incredulous.

"Think like a shoofly," Nick said. "That's what my phone call with Oliver was all about. He laid it on me straight. Lousy timing, you know—coming up in the middle of the Internal Affairs investigation . . ."

"They think you cut a deal with Sato?" Charlie said, really disgusted. "But I can back you up!"

Nick was listening to something—a far-off sound coming rapidly closer. Motorcycles. In a minute, six bikers loomed up, owning the street with the arrogance and energy of young men with power between their legs.

"They'll believe what they want to believe," he told Charlie wearily. "Welcome to the shitstorm."

The bikers headed straight for them, laughing loudly, jeering. The motors roared deafeningly as they split at the last possible second, two of the bikes jumping the curb as their riders whooped with glee. In a minute they were gone, and the streets were silent again except for the sound of the wind beating against the paper lanterns, rustling the wind chimes.

Nick and Charlie stood in the middle of the street, in the middle of the night, in the middle of Asia, realizing just how far from home they were.

And then a miracle came along in the shape of an empty taxi. The driver was probably on his way home, but when two wild *gaigins* leaped out into the street in front of him, he had to slam on the brakes to avoid running them down. Shaking with terror, the driver tried to snap the all-doors lock, but the barbarians knew that trick and opened the back door so quickly he was prevented from doing so. They climbed into his taxi, baggage and all, and the younger *gaigin* spoke some foreign words, over and over again, so many times that they began to sound like the name of Meiji. Perhaps they wanted the shrine? But the gates were closed at this hour of night. The district, then. Perhaps the hotel. He would take them there and plead with the doormen to relieve him of this onerous burden. He hoped the two ranting Americans, who became instantly subdued when they climbed into his taxi, were not too drunk to pay.

Charlie slept deeply from the minute he hit the hard narrow bed. Nick smoked and paced and stared out the window as the last act of the neon light show closed.

They were at the Prefecture headquarters by one minute to nine. Masahiro greeted them politely, if not exactly enthusiastically.

"I have taken the liberty of ordering breakfast for you," he told them, rising from his desk in the bullpen. He came around into the aisle. "It will be brought to us downstairs in the file room. If you will follow me?"

He led them into a room that could have been in any police station in the world. Rows of green metal filing cabinets crisscrossed the room, with small tables set every few yards down the narrow aisles, each with two straight chairs and a reading light. An officer sat at one of the tables, poring over a file while chopsticking food into his mouth from a bowl held with his other hand.

Masahiro led them to a row of files and drew up an extra chair at one of the tables. He opened a drawer and withdrew a thick folder which he laid on the table. Just at that moment, the old woman who had brought lunch the day before appeared with her steaming baskets and set out bowls and chopsticks for them.

"That looks good," Charlie said. "What is this called?"

"That is *bento*," Masahiro told him. "Tofu skins, fermented soybeans, *umebosahi* . . . I hope you like it. I believe it is more to the Western taste than this humble rice porridge that I eat."

"Oh, yeah, yeah, sure. Sounds delicious." Charlie grinned and started trying to juggle the chopsticks in some way that would allow the runny mess to get near his mouth. Nick ignored the food. He was turning over photos of Sato, studying each one carefully.

There he was at about sixteen, in an ill-fitting tuxedo, surrounded by laughing girls in formal gowns. There was an astonishing black-and-white photo of Sato stripped to the waist, revealing his upper body covered with tattoos. He was squatting in a weight lifter's pose and showing off his muscles as well as his illustrations. There were quite a few photos like that—Sato in *sumo*-wrestling drag, Sato stripped down and posing with a *samurai* sword held high over his head, Sato flexing his muscles in a windstorm on the parapet atop a high building.

"Looks like we got a real nut case," Nick said.

"Sato Koji," Masahiro filled in. "He started young and rose fast," he told them, between loud slurps of his porridge. Fumbling with the chopsticks, Charlie finally managed to shovel the food from the bowl to his mouth. "Sato began as a street enforcer, soon became a minor boss."

As Nick had demanded, the text of the files had been translated overnight. He picked up the summary sheet and ran down it quickly. "Dime-a-dance hitter goes made man, controls the docks and some construction in Hawaii."

"Don't you like the *bento?*" Masahiro asked him politely.

It crossed Nick's mind that maybe he was getting his string jerked. He took a long sardonic look at Masahiro, whose face, as always, was giving nothing away. "No, it's fabulous," he assured the assistant inspector. "Smells like Bayonne at low tide."

Masahiro didn't understand the words but he was subtly pleased that Nick Conklin found the breakfast not to his taste.

"We know the victim last night was Sato's man," Nick said.

"Right," Charlie agreed.

Heavy footsteps sounded in the corridor. Probably morning change-up, Nick thought.

Reading from the file, Nick said, "And three days ago, Sato's suspected of hitting Ok-a-da Gen-kuro. Right?"

Pronouncing it differently, Masahiro repeated the name. "Okada Genkuro," he said. "Damascene maker, an artist."

"Yeah, an engraver," Nick said. "So Sato hops a plane and forty-eight hours later he's snapping caps at Scalari's."

Masahiro thought for a moment. "Fifty-four hours later," he said. Nick eyed him quickly, but there was no sign that Masahiro was anything but earnestly trying to be helpful. Nick and Charlie exchanged a weary glance.

"Who's this monkey with Sato in all these pictures?" Charlie asked. "Looks like he's been careless with matches."

The photos were taken by surveillance cameras, and the quality was grainy and not always in focus. The dates stamped on the edges were no more recent than five years ago. Most were black-and-white, a few in color. All showed Sato with a grotesquely scarred man, burn marks disfiguring his face and hands.

Outside in the hall, there were more footsteps, and it was beginning to sound like an army assembling for a battle. Charlie put the photos down on the table and got up, as if to stretch. He took a step or two toward the door.

"That is Kunio Sugai," Masahiro said. He spoke slowly, as if hesitating for some reason. "He was burned in American firebombing. April 1945. It took his father and his brother."

Nick nodded curtly. "What were the two of them doing together?" he asked.

"Sato was Sugai's lieutenant once, about five years ago."

"Cut the bullshit," Nick said abruptly. "There's a war going on between the two of them. You're not planning to tell me anything about that?" Under his breath, he muttered, "Fucking suit!"

Now excited voices could be heard out in the corridor as well as marching feet. Charlie opened the door a crack. A pair of armed and uniformed officers marched past, in a hurry to get somewhere.

"Hey, what's with the marines?" he asked Masahiro.

Masahiro shrugged, clearly uncomfortable. "A drill. Training, perhaps," he lied.

Charlie shook his head. His hand stayed on the doorknob. "You've got to start cutting us in on this stuff, Masa," he said.

Nick was staring at the photos, and off on his own track. "What the hell could have been in that box?" he mused. He looked down at the scarred man. "This Sugai—was he into drugs?"

"No," Masahiro said firmly. "Steel, liquor, horses. He owns part of Club Miyako. Then there's guns, prostitution. He's a very powerful *Oyabun*. Head of the *Izaki-gunmi.*"

"Hey, Nick," Charlie said, opening the door wider. "Look at this."

Nick got up and joined him at the door. Three or four SWAT officers ran past, carrying sledgehammers with both hands in front of them. They held out their hands as they jogged past a ranking officer who was handing out packets of live ammo from a carton held by a noncom.

"Sledgehammers? Live ammunition?" Nick turned to glare at Masahiro. "Training?" he yelped.

Charlie grabbed his jacket off the back of the chair. Masahiro was looking exceedingly uncomfortable. Shifty, you might say.

"Masahiro, what the hell is going on?" Nick asked him.

"They have a tip about Sato's last hideout," Masahiro explained reluctantly. "Only a tip. I promise to keep you informed as they find out anything more."

Nick nodded. "Do you have the file on Sugai?" he asked, as if accepting Masahiro's terms.

"Yes." Masahiro turned to the filing cabinet and before he knew it Nick and Charlie were out the door.

12

Masahiro cursed roundly and started after them, stopped himself and grabbed for the phone. Then, uncharacteristically, he opted to skip the authorization and dropped the phone back on its hook. He grabbed his briefcase and tore out the door and down the hall past the startled officer with his hand still out to distribute the live ammo. Faster on his feet than his years in a desk chair might suggest, Masahiro worked his way through the troops lined up to board the police bus, shoved his way to the head of the line and then onto the bus. Sure enough, his terrible Americans had found themselves a couple of seats about halfway back. They sat, arms crossed, clearly unmovable, in the midst of the stone-faced, heavily armed assault team.

He made his way down the narrow aisle of the bus. "You cannot do this," he told them quietly, not wanting to lose face but knowing his words would have no effect.

"No shit," Charlie commented.

"Please, gentlemen," Masahiro implored. "I need authorization."

"This one's New York style, Masa," Nick said.

Charlie nodded. "First we do, then we go get authorization," he explained.

Suddenly the door was slammed shut and the police bus lurched into gear, throwing Masahiro off-balance. He grabbed the back of a seat and looked around quickly to see if anyone smiled, but the soldiers sat immobile, holding their weapons and thinking their own thoughts. There wasn't a damn thing Masahiro could do now except squeeze onto the seat between the two devils who had been sent to plague his golden years.

The bus was escorted by two police cars with full sirens blazing, as they careened through the streets at racing speed. The bus bounced and jounced, and just as Charlie was beginning to really regret the *bento* he had managed to get down his gullet, they screeched to a stop.

They were in front of a pachinko parlor, a storefront featuring row after row of coin-operated games not too different from pinball machines. Instead of five or six steel balls, hundreds of tiny pellets rained through vertical mazes in intricate patterns. People stood at pachinko machines by the hour, putting in coins and watching the steel pellets fly. Only in this place, there were no players to be seen.

The assault team deployed from the bus into the emptied storefront, and the cops who had cleared it now stood respectfully aside as the team rushed in, guns and sledgehammers at the ready. One group split off and headed for the rear entrance to the building. Charlie and Nick followed Masahiro inside the pachinko parlor, behind the troops who raced through the cleared narrow aisles toward a staircase near the back of the room.

As they approached the stairs, the rear door burst open and the raiding parties converged from front and rear. They charged up the stairs. Nick and Charlie started up, but Masahiro jumped to stop them, blocking the way, standing facing them with his arms folded across his chest.

"Observers," he said firmly. They had never seen him look so fierce.

When you're right, you're right. "Okay, boss," Nick agreed.

There was a closed door at the top of the stairs. Apparently it was locked, too, although the team didn't wait for a key—two burly officers attacked it with crunching blows from their sledgehammers. The door collapsed like splintered cardboard, and wood slivers exploded in all directions. The armed men stormed into the upper room.

By the time Nick and Charlie and Masahiro got inside, five very surprised gonzos were already in custody. They were bare-chested, and every one was covered with tattoos, but none of them was Sato.

The room was large and casually furnished with comfortable chairs and low tables where tea might be served. There were desks and filing cabinets, too—this was a combination office and living room. A small kitchen area could be seen off to one side, and there was a door leading to a bedroom and john.

The five suspects were being lined up against a wall,

and the officers were checking their identification papers. Walking over for a closer look, Nick spotted a too-familiar suit and tie neatly hung over a chair in the corner. He had spent a lot of hours on a cramped airplane sitting next to that suit.

"The son of a bitch was here, Charlie," he said.

Masahiro was sticking to them like flypaper. Nick walked over to the lineup, where all the tattooed wonders were standing with their hands behind them, their dark heads hanging down. One of them was practically doing deep bends to keep from letting anyone see his face. Nick came closer and took a good look. It was one of the fake cops from the airport. The SWAT who was frisking him called him Katayama.

"Hello again, darling," Nick said.

Katayama lifted his head, smiled sardonically, and spit. It landed on Nick's cheek. Unsurprised, Nick turned to Charlie, as if to say: hey, did you catch this guy's act? Katayama let down his guard for an instant, and in that flash Nick turned, grabbed him by the throat, and shoved him with full angry strength slam-up against the wall.

Masahiro yelped. "Detective Conklin!" He tried to pull Nick off, but Nick ignored him. His face inches away from Katayama's, he repeated, "Hello *again*, darling. Where's your boss?"

Masahiro yanked at Nick but Nick held Katayama pressed to the wall in a death grip. Then all at once members of the assault team were all over Nick, and they forced him back. Everybody was shouting excitedly in Japanese, including Charlie, who didn't speak the language. But it sounded right, as he scrambled and yanked and punched and tugged to pull the cops off Nick.

Masahiro led them away to a far corner and insisted they sit down.

"Let me talk to him for five minutes," Nick pleaded.

"It's not proper," Masahiro told him sternly. "You're a foreigner."

"We speak the international language," Charlie said wryly.

"This isn't New York, Detective," Masahiro said. "We have rules here."

"Rules?" Nick retorted. "I've got news for you, Matsumoto. I've seen Sato's work. He doesn't follow the program."

"You must learn patience," Masahiro told them.

"Fuck patience," Nick said. "It's for old maids, *Inspector.*"

Masahiro sighed. "You want to observe," he said, "observe. If not, leave." He waited for them to answer him.

Tucking his shirt back inside his sweater, Nick agreed, temporarily at least. "You're the boss, Masa," he said. He and Charlie turned their attention from the suspects to the room itself, which Osaka's finest were turning out with methodical precision.

Everything was being dusted for fingerprints. Files were opened and their contents were examined by white-gloved officers. Sheets of plastic were laid out on the floor, onto which the contents of cartons and boxes and wastebaskets were dumped. Everything was closely sifted and labeled. Charlie's eye caught something yellow—tissue-thin paper that fit the description of the wrapping paper last seen in Scalari's Bar and Ristorante in New York City, U.S.A.

"Nicky," Charlie said. Nick glanced at him and

followed his eyes toward the odds and ends being spilled out onto the plastic. He didn't see what Charlie was looking at, not at first. "The paper the box was wrapped in?" Charlie prompted, and then Nick saw the distinctive bright yellow color standing out from all the other papers in the room.

He got up from his chair, stretching.

"Where you going?" Masahiro asked apprehensively.

"Just going to have a look around, promise not to touch anything or punch anybody. You can watch me from there. I'll be good, Masa. Just want to see if there's anything I recognize, okay?"

"Okay," Masahiro said reluctantly.

Nick went across the room to the officer who was sifting the contents of a wastebasket he'd just turned out. He looked down and then winked back at Charlie. It was the same yellow paper. The cop growled something guttural, and probably none too polite, at Nick, and he backed off.

"Okay, boss, stay placid," he told the cop.

Another contingent of cops came through the splintered remains of the door—led by Superintendent Ohashi. Two uniformed officers flanked him, not the ones who had been in his office earlier. Nick flashed a glance back at Masahiro, who had gone quite pale at the sight of his superior. Masahiro leaped up from his seat and headed for Nick, but he was too late. Ohashi spotted Masahiro and called out to him imperiously. Masahiro stopped in his tracks. He was in deep shit.

From across the room, Ohashi's voice rang out harsh and punitive. Nick had been in this country just barely long enough to know that raised voices and a public chewing-out were a lot more humiliating here than they would be back home, where everybody hollered all the time. It was heavy here, and he almost felt sorry for poor old suit-and-tie Masahiro. Almost.

Most of the cops in the room were trying not to look at Masahiro and Ohashi, but a ponderous silence had fallen over the room and the unusual confrontation was drawing serious interest. Nick moved to the table where the suspects' wallets were being examined. The contents were laid out neatly and the cop in charge was listing everything on a police form. Six of the items were crisp American one-hundred-dollar bills. Nick waited until the cop couldn't resist a sneaky glance over toward Ohashi and Masahiro. In a flash, Nick pocketed a fistful of the bills.

Gesturing to Charlie, Nick headed for the door. What he didn't know was that Masahiro, backed up in a corner, suffering the humiliation of this public dressing-down and vowing to himself to have revenge on the Americans for putting him in this position, was keeping one eye on Nick over Ohashi's shoulder, and he saw what Nick had done.

13

Nick and Charlie walked downstairs and through the empty pachinko parlor.

"Got something?" Charlie asked him.

"Maybe," Nick said. They walked out of the storefront and came onto the sidewalk, which had started to crowd up with curious citizens.

"If you got good news," Charlie told him glumly, "it would be nice to share it with Masa. I think he's in deep with the boss."

Nick's main priority at that moment was not saving Masahiro's ass. He kept moving on through the crowd with Charlie close behind him. They didn't notice a black Suzuki bike on the street or the rider all dressed in black from helmet to studded boots who watched the two Americans with more than passing interest. Sato's face was hidden behind the one-way glass of his visor; he could see them but they could have no idea who it was they passed directly in front of. When they reached the other side of the street, Sato gunned the bike and sped off in the other direction.

They came to a fast-noodle stand, an open counter set back from the sidewalk with an awning offering a quiet place to stop for a moment. The breakfast crowds had dwindled and the lunch-hour rush had yet to begin, so they had the place pretty much to themselves.

Nick pulled one of the crisp hundred-dollar bills from his pocket. He rubbed it reverently between his thumb and two fingers, then he rolled and unrolled it in the palm of his hand while Charlie watched, for once struck speechless. Nick stuck a cigarette in his mouth and lit it. Instead of putting the Zippo away, he touched the flame to the corner of the bill. They both watched closely as the money burned.

Paydirt.

"Hey, we're getting to know our way around this burg," Charlie said, as they strode into police head-quarters about a half-hour later. They had both been a lot more observant of the route they had taken this morning in the police bus than they had the night before. There wasn't going to be a ride or a walk anyplace in this country in the near future that these two couldn't trace their steps back from, and without leaving a trail of bread crumbs, either.

As they hurried up the steps and into the reception area, they caught a glimpse of Katayama and the other four prisoners being booked and escorted to a holding pen.

"Think they'll get anything out of him?" Charlie asked.

"Oh, sure, it's the polite approach," Nick muttered. "First they'll have tea and then maybe they'll chat. Bowing all the way, of course."

They went on up to the bullpen, but Masahiro's desk was empty.

"Where's the assistant inspector?" Charlie asked the secretary.

The man nodded and smiled.

With gestures, shrugs, hand signals, and facial tics, repeating "Masahiro, Masahiro," they finally managed to get their message across, and the secretary smiled even wider and began to explain something in rapid Japanese. Since that didn't work, he tried charades, gesturing wildly and repeating a sound effect like "Katakatakatakataka."

"He's working on the railroad?" Charlie guessed.

"Target range?" Nick tried. "Baseball?"

"He's a riveter!" they crowed simultaneously.

They left the bullpen no wiser than they had come in. Walking down the long corridor, Nick suddenly stopped. "Listen!" he said. Charlie listened.

It was a sound very much like the noise the secretary had been making, coming from the other end of the hall. They checked it out—a door opened onto a gym with a highly polished floor and a class of twenty identically dressed men practicing moves with *kendo* sticks. As they clashed the sticks in a series of intricate moves, something like fencing, the sound was their clue—the secretary had been trying to tell them that Masahiro was here. But which one was he? They all wore masks with visors.

One of the spectators came rushing over to them as soon as they stepped inside. Pointing excitedly, he let them know that they were to remove their shoes and leave them in the rows of other discarded footwear just inside the door.

"I think I got a hole in my sock," Nick confessed as he pulled off his sneakers.

"I'm embarrassed to be seen with you," Charlie said.

They stood watching the elaborate moves of the *kendo* game, as the instructor called out commands. They tried to figure out which one was Masahiro. This was no time for a fitness class, or the precinct championship games, or whatever the hell this was.

"Hey, where's my man, Masahiro?" Charlie called out to a couple of the players as they leaped and sashayed close to them. "Love the turtle suits, fellas," he added.

Nick shouted just loudly enough for Masahiro to hear, if he was there. "Come on, buddy! We've got news!"

A few *kendo* players were resting on the sidelines, with their helmets and sticks on the floor beside them. Charlie couldn't resist picking up one of the sticks. The onlookers were not amused; he got glowering looks but, so far as he could tell for certain, no overt threats.

The class continued to move in unison—almost a military ballet. The instructor called out incisive commands and they were executed sharply. Suddenly another voice called out, almost in agony.

"I will have no more to do with you! Get out!"

It was Masahiro's voice as he passed close by them. He was proclaiming a wish, a prayer, a vow, and a desperate promise from the bottom of his heart.

At a command from the leader, the class broke into sets of two and faced off, preparing for individual fencing. Some of them stepped out of the group, removing their face coverings. Masahiro was one of them. Nick and Charlie crossed the slippery gym floor in their stocking-feet to get to him.

"Look," Nick said, "I know you took some heat for taking us to the raid—"

"Superintendent Ohashi is waiting for you in his office," Masahiro interrupted coldly.

"Masa, it's okay. You're covered, man," Charlie reassured him. "We're going up to square you with Ohashi right now. Okay?"

Masahiro turned without a word and took off. Charlie and Nick looked at each other.

"Jesus," Nick shouted after him. "Would you listen up!"

Masahiro kept walking across the gym floor toward the exit. Nick grabbed the *kendo* stick out of Charlie's hand and took off after him. He got close enough to tap Masahiro on the thigh with the stick.

"Hey, drop the hard-on, man, and let me explain," he said.

Masahiro stopped and glared back at Nick. "You have dishonored me and the rest of our department," he said. "You're a thief. I saw you take the money."

"Some thief," Nick grunted. "It's the only way I can get anything done in this department. You guys won't let me wipe my ass without making three phone calls!"

Masahiro kept on walking. Nick rapped him again with the stick.

"Hey, hey, I'm talking to you!"

"I have informed Superintendent Ohashi of your crime. He has spoken to your superiors in New York.

We know the kind of man you are," Masahiro said coldly.

Nick couldn't believe this guy—he would fit right in with the folks on Internal Affairs back home. "You stupid bastard," he shouted. "You don't know day one about me. Your self-righteous bullshit is going to get us kicked out of here!"

That was it. Masahiro was as fast and light as a hummingbird. He knocked the weapon from Nick's hand, and with a guttural shout he swung his own stick down, stopping a hairsbreadth from splitting open Nick's head.

Nick held his hands up. "All right, you win," he gasped.

Masahiro momentarily relaxed his guard. Nick's reflexive move was learned on the street, but it was as fast and flashy as it gets. The unexpected kick and a single hand chop sent Masahiro, in all his armor and protective covering, sprawling on the floor.

Nick stood over him. "Lesson one," he said. "Don't pull it if you're not going to use it."

He started toward the door. In the next instant, his nose was butting against the hard varnish of the gym floor. Masahiro sat heavily on his shoulders, his arms were pinned behind him, and the gentlemen of the *kendo* class were cheering with unseemly enthusiasm. It was enough to make a guy feel unwelcome.

14

*P*erhaps a theft by a police officer is taken for granted in your country—" Superintendent Ohashi began, but Nick cut him off.

"There was a hundred-dollar bill in the victim's mouth at Club Miyako. Sato killed an engraver before he went to New York. The box? Samples, maybe, or plates. Either way, your war is over counterfeiting. And we could have rolled on this a long time ago, if you didn't treat us like enemies."

He had Ohashi's full attention, and Masahiro's, too. He pulled one of the bills from his pocket and held it up in the air. "One time only," Nick told him, "so come down out of the cheap seats."

The superintendent got up from his leather chair and stood behind his desk, waiting, with a this-had-better-be-very-good expression on his face. Masahiro, still in his full *kendo* regalia except for the mask, stood to one side watching warily.

Nick pulled out his Zippo and flicked on the flame. "Watch and learn," he said, setting fire to the bill. "Look. The impression barely rises above the ash. Here . . . and here. Not made under enough pressure, or it would be higher. It's good stuff. The best I've seen, but it's not money."

He blew out the flame and tossed the charred phoney bill into Ohashi's wastebasket. He turned to go and stopped in front of Masahiro. Jabbing a finger into the assistant inspector's padded chest guard, he spelled out the words like bullets. "You got a problem, you bring it to your partner, not the suits, scumbag."

He walked out of Ohashi's office. Charlie felt kind of sorry for Masahiro. After all, he figured, the guy was just doing his job the way they'd probably taught him—different cultures, different cops. "We were going to tell you, man," he tried to explain over his shoulder as he hurried after Nick.

They passed the holding area on their way out, and just for the hell of it, Nick opened the door and took a look inside. Katayama was still there, sitting on a straight chair and staring at the wall, waiting for processing.

Charlie stopped at the doorway, but Nick walked in. The thug looked scared and very, very surprised. Nick slapped him once, hard, backhanded, across the Adam's apple. Katayama gasped loudly for breath, his mouth open like a fish. Nick reached in his pocket for his last phony hundred-dollar bill. It crackled as he wadded it up and shoved it between Katayama's rotten teeth.

"Tell Sato I raise him this," Nick said.

He strode out of the room and they headed for the fresh air.

"What's that all about?" Charlie asked.

"From his lips to Sato's ears." Nick was striding down the street as if he'd lived in this precinct all his life.

"Where're we heading, boss?"

"Hotel. Shit, shine, shower and shave. Then I want to talk to a lady," Nick said.

"How about some *food* while we're at it?" Charlie suggested.

"I'll eat anything that's not moving," Nick agreed.

"Well, now *that* I can't guarantee." Charlie laughed. "Do slimy noodles count?"

Several hours later, rested and refreshed, they found their way back to the Club Miyako. It was early evening and the lights were already ablaze in the streets. Clusters of office workers were pouring out of the skyscrapers and heading for the bars, shops were crowded, and more than once Nick and Charlie took pity on their tail and waited for him to catch up. Masahiro stayed well behind them, but he was pathetically obvious.

As they neared the club, Charlie turned back and caught Masahiro's eye. The assistant inspector was mortified and tried to shield his face with his hands, turning to look at an exhibit of plastic food in a restaurant window.

"I think we embarrass him," Charlie said.

"A real shamus," Nick commented.

They went into the club. What a difference from the somber atmosphere of the night before! Now the place was really jumping. Most of the customers were salarymen in groups, apparently determined to get as drunk as possible as loudly as possible. Hostesses fastened themselves to the customers in the booths and at the bar. On the stage, a management-level suit was giving the *karaoke* a workout, to the riotous amusement of his friends.

The *karaoke* is to modern Japanese bars what dart games have been to English pubs for centuries—everyone has to try it, and it becomes some kind of test of manhood, talent, nerve, humor, degree of drunkenness, and a whole host of other things. The *karaoke* is an electronic toy which not only amplifies the voice but also magically mixes the sounds of prerecorded music with the voice, much like an expensive recording studio. The words to the song are projected across a television monitor for the benefit of the performer, who sings into the microphone, under the spotlight, and comes out sounding like a pro whether he can carry a tune or not. It's a toss-up who has the most fun, the performers or the audience.

Charlie and Nick sat in a booth. Immediately, two smiling hostesses joined them.

"My name Norie," said the one who snuggled up to Charlie.

"Well, hi, there, Norie," Charlie said. "You speak English?"

"Oh, yes, very good English," Norie said proudly. "My friend speaks no English, but I translate." She giggled. "Except I think you don't need translating."

The girl who had glued herself to Nick just giggled and put her hand on his knee.

Masahiro came in and sat at the bar with his back to them.

"Should we put him out of his misery?" Charlie suggested.

Nick just shrugged. He was still in a sour mood despite the nap and shower, and he was ignoring the girl who clung to his arm. "Well, the menu's half in English, anyway," he said. "There's even a couple of things I recognize. Shrimp cocktail, for starters." A waitress came over and took their order.

"What's a Hurricane Special Cocktail?" Charlie asked her. The waitress, with Norie's help, explained that it came in a tall glass, was pink and yellow, had seven kinds of liquor in it, and came with a paper umbrella and a maraschino cherry. "Sounds just perfect," Charlie said. Nick raised his eyebrows. But then his face softened into a grin when Charlie added, "See that man at the bar—the middle-aged fellow, kind of tall, stocky build? He's drinking *sake?* Tell the bartender to give him a Hurricane Special, with our compliments. Okay?"

The girls asked for champagne but seemed perfectly happy to settle for beer. When the shrimp came, it was raw. Some of the tails were still flapping.

"Hey, one of you pixies got a spear?" Charlie asked the girls. "This stuff is hopping all over my plate."

Norie giggled. "It tastes better when it's squirming," she said.

Nick leaned over to her. "Honey," he said, "you're the only person I've met in this country so far who's got a grip on reality."

The *karaoke* singer was doing a hideously off-key Japanese version of the old Frank Sinatra song "High Hopes." The volume was turned way up.

"Hey, a little mercy back here!" Charlie called out. "People are eating!"

Nick spoke quietly, going under the racket instead of trying to outshout it. "Norie, right?" he asked the girl across the table. She nodded brightly. "That American woman, name of Joyce? You know her?"

Norie looked blank. If she knew, she wasn't giving anything away. "Tall? Blond?" Nick persisted. "Is she working tonight?"

Charlie tried to help out. "Ass like a perfect teardrop," he told Norie, who laughed and put her free arm around his shoulders. Charlie kept looking over at the bar, and now he said, "Look, he's getting it."

The bartender had set the ridiculous drink in front of Masahiro. They saw the bartender motion toward their booth, but Masahiro did not turn around to look at them.

Like a toothache letting up, the song ended. Charlie took advantage of the momentary peace after the raucous applause to yell across the room, "Hey, Masa! Come on over!"

They saw his shoulders heave as he sighed. Caught. He dug in his pocket, left some money on the bar, and came toward them carrying the huge glass with the tropical drink and little paper umbrella. He looked like he had had a few already.

He stood looking down at Nick. "Big shot from New York," he said, slurring his words a little.

"Matsumoto of the Mounties," Nick countered. "Did somebody tell you to tail me in case I was about to steal the silverware?"

Masahiro pulled himself up to his full dignity. "Superintendent Ohashi would like to see you in the morning," he said.

Nick nodded. "I'll check my book." He cocked his

thumb over his shoulder toward the exit. "Bye, Masa, you've delivered your message."

"Hey, hang on," Charlie intervened. "Everybody did the right thing. You did, Nick, and you did too, Masa. No more, guys, okay? Sit down, Masa. Smoke the pipe, Nick."

They both thought it over for an instant or two, and then Masahiro settled into the booth alongside Charlie. He looked straight ahead, avoiding Nick's gaze. The *karaoke* started again, and it was "High Hopes" again, with a different suit up there making an ass of himself for his pals. This one's voice was no truer than the other's, and the volume was just as loud. Almost imperceptibly, Masahiro's hand started tapping in time with the rhythm.

"You like this stuff?" Charlie asked him.

"Oh, yes," Masahiro said. "'High Hopes.' I was a teenager when it was new." He started humming along with the music.

Charlie grinned. "Give the man a few drinks and he's a guest on 'American Bandstand.'" He laughed.

Still facing straight ahead, Masahiro switched abruptly to the subject that was foremost on his mind, and on Nick's. "I did my duty, Conklin," he said. "These are the men I work for."

"In my local you got a problem, you bring it to your partner, not the suits," Nick told him.

Masahiro finally looked at him. "Perhaps you should think less of yourself and more of your group," he said. "Learn to work like a Japanese." He looked at the girl clinging to Nick's side. "You've already learned how to relax like a Japanese," he commented dryly. He went back to humming with the music.

When Nick didn't say anything, Masahiro went on.

It was the *sake* and the Hurricane Special, but it was interesting to hear him open up for a change, Charlie thought. "I grew up with your soldiers," he said. "You were a wise people then. But now . . . music and clothes are all America is good for. We make the machines. We have built the future. You were powerful but . . ." He downed the last of the Special. The paper umbrella rode the liquid all the way to the bottom of the glass. "But we won the peace," Masahiro finished.

Nick leaned forward. "Yeah, and if any one of you ever had an original idea, you'd get so uptight you'd yank yourselves up your own asshole," he retorted.

"Hey, what is this?" Charlie protested. "You guys in a massive conspiracy to fuck up my evening?" He returned Norie's squeeze. Masahiro and Nick fell silent.

"Yo, Nick," Charlie said. Nick followed Charlie's glance across the room. The tall beautiful blonde was introducing a young hostess to a businessman sitting alone in a booth. The man reached up for Joyce and she bent down so he could whisper something in her ear. She laughed.

Nick peeled the girl from his side and got up and walked over to Joyce.

"Always works," he said in the blonde's pearly ear. "Little dab'll do ya."

Joyce turned and stared at him. "The peroxide," he reminded her. "Got a few seconds?"

"I'm with clients," she said. The color of her hair was extraordinary in these surroundings, or maybe it would have been that way anywhere in the world. It was all honey and sunshine, piled up in a wispy almost old-fashioned sweep, although there was nothing else old-fashioned about her. She was a knockout and she looked like nothing had surprised her in a long, long time. Again he found himself wondering what the hell she was doing in Osaka, Japan. She brushed past him.

He stuck with her as she moved through the crowded room. "Chicago," he pleaded, "listen, my balls are in the wringer and I need help from someone who speaks the language. Please."

Joyce ignored him and joined a booth filled with jolly suits and ties. To their surprise, Nick slid into the booth right next to her.

"Turn your meter over," he said. "My money's as good as theirs."

The businessmen were feeling no pain and they seemed to find Nick very amusing. One beefy fellow made a few very readable gestures indicating that they knew exactly who he was. They all roared with drunken hilarity. Nick smiled and put his arm around the shoulders of the joker who had started the laughter. The man recoiled from his touch.

"I'm sorry, fellas, the young lady can't play with you now." He held up his police I.D. "You'll just have to play with yourselves," he said.

"Jesus . . ." Joyce groaned.

The businessman directed a sharp comment at Nick, and his buddies stopped laughing abruptly. Things could get ugly all of a sudden. Joyce said something in Japanese to appease the guy, and then she turned quickly back to Nick.

"There's a girl at the bar," she said, "wearing a sequined dress. Give her fifty dollars and go where she takes you."

Nick nodded his thanks and got up from the booth,

much to everyone's relief. Joyce said something to make them all smile again. Nick headed for the bar.

The girl in the sequined dress was there, all right. She was the same stunning beauty he had seen the night before, only now the dress was a different color and this time she wasn't all splattered with blood.

15

*T*he later the hour, the drunker the patrons, the more awful the antics with the *karaoke*. As inhibitions dropped away, singers got bolder and sillier. But what the hell. Charlie and his good friend Masahiro clinked their *sake* cups and toasted each other with the good hot wine.

"Up and down," said Masahiro.

"Kampai," said Charlie. Down the hatch.

He leaned over to confide in his pal under the dreadful din of amplified amateur night. "Listen, Masa, you want to hang around with the NYPD, there is one thing you're gonna have to do."

Drunk but instantly defensive, Masahiro reared back. "What?"

Charlie put his arm around Masahiro's shoulder. "We're gonna have to lose the K-mart tie. It's a fire hazard," he said. He loosened his own tie and undid the knot, handed it to his new friend. "Here."

Masahiro drained the tiny cup of *sake,* then set it down on the table, reached up to unknot his tie and slip it off. He quickly tied Charlie's tie around his neck and admired his reflection as well as he could on the back of a spoon. It was a huge hit with the two hostesses.

"It's top drawer," Masahiro said, pleased. "Yes?"

Charlie nodded and smiled. "It's you," he said. "You've already upped your percentage," he told Norie and her friend. The singing was getting on his nerves, though. "Hey, meatball." He heckled the crooner who was currently on stage. "If you can't hit the note, throw a hat at it!"

"You could do better?" Masahiro asked him.

"I cannot tell a lie," Charlie nodded modestly.

"Then," Masahiro said cheerfully, "put it up or shut it up."

Charlie thought it over for a second. "All right, wise guy," he told Masahiro. "Maybe it's time someone planted the flag in this joint." He struggled to his feet and Masahiro grinned happily from ear to ear, sitting back to anticipate his young American friend making an asshole of himself just like everyone else. He laughed and took another cupful of *sake.*

But instead of heading for the stage, Charlie reached for Masahiro's arm and yanked him out of the booth. Before he could figure out what hit him, Masahiro was being hustled toward the stage and the *karaoke.*

"What are you doing? Charlie . . . stop!"

* * *

There was an isolated booth near the annex that had a commanding view of the main room; you could sit there and see without being seen. The young woman with the slinky sequins had taken Nick there, and he sat waiting, although he didn't know what he was waiting for. The girl either couldn't or wouldn't understand anything he had said to her. He sat alone, with an ancient pack of playing cards backed with *samurai* warriors, and he played solitaire while keeping an eye on the action on the floor. Every now and then a hostess would bring him a drink, but she didn't offer to sit with him. The ashtray filled up and overflowed.

He played an ace of diamonds all the way up to the jack and got stuck. Then what he had hoped would happen happened—Joyce slid into the booth opposite him. She had a really nice, friendly mouth when she smiled.

"Hi," he said.

The smile disappeared. It was lecture time. "You're stubborn, dangerous, and too stupid to know it," she told him. "Why don't you just buy yourself some souvenirs and go on back to New York?"

Nick shuffled the cards. "You give great advice when you're not pushing drinks and waving your ass like the flag on the Fourth of July." He shuffled some more. He looked at her appreciatively, up and down and up again. "Work pay for a dress like that?" he asked pointedly.

She didn't take offense. She didn't even get miffed. "Don't break into a sweat," she told him evenly. "You don't know a damn thing about what I do. I pour their drinks, listen to their troubles, and go home alone.

Unless I don't want to. Talking to you is about as close to a compromise as I get."

Nick laughed. She could not only take it but she could hand it right back. He liked that fine. "All right, maybe I was out of line down there," he said, nodding toward the main floor. "But I had a feeling you wouldn't give me your home address." He dealt a hand of blackjack. "How about one hand, loser becomes a soft touch?" he suggested.

Joyce started to smile, but she was cut off by a crackling blare of static. She reached into her little beaded bag and took out a walkie-talkie. The static became rapid-fire Japanese, and she answered in a fast and businesslike tone that impressed Nick in spite of himself.

"Roku ban e annai shite. Sugu ikukara," she said. The static said *"Hai"* and abruptly cut off. Joyce stashed the machine back in her little purse.

"I gotta ask. What was that?" Nick said.

"I said 'put them at table six, I'll be right down,'" Joyce told him. "Look, if you're looking for Sato, I can't help you. He hasn't been here in over a year. He got rough with some of the girls."

Nick dealt her another card and then one to himself, turned over his hole card. She had a seven showing, he had two eights. "Who did he see regularly?" he asked her.

"What makes you think I'd pay attention?" Joyce retorted.

Nick looked her in the eyes. They were terrifically blue and calm and clear, and he liked the way they looked back without telling much. "I think you'd notice if one of your regulars came in with a new tie," he told her.

Joyce smiled in spite of herself. "He had a different girl every time," she told him. "I don't know anyone who still sees him, if that's where you're heading."

"And Sugai?" Nick asked.

She didn't answer that one.

"He owns a piece of this place, right?" Nick pressed her. "How can I get to him?"

Joyce shook her head. "Look," she tried to explain, "I've been here seven years and I still can't read the headlines. There's three different ways of saying hello, five different bows, and you need a manual to read smiles. Yes means no. And maybe means never."

"You didn't answer my question," Nick persisted.

"Let the police handle it," she advised him earnestly. "No one's going to help a *gaigin.*"

"Gaigin?"

"A foreigner. Stranger. Barbarian. Me. You." She smiled faintly. "More you," she added.

Nick laughed. He offered the deck of cards. "Take another. Trust me."

She nodded absently and he dealt her another card, facedown. "Did you know they got lights at Wrigley Field now?" he told her.

That got to her. She searched his eyes to see what the gag was. "Bullshit," she said.

Nick nodded and crossed his heart with his index finger.

"Since when?" she asked wistfully. Her walkie-talkie sputtered again. "I have to go," she said.

As she stood up she glanced out over the floor and something in her eyes made Nick look, too. There was Sugai—you couldn't miss his scarred face—and the girl in the splashy sequins. She was clutching his arm as if she had a right to it, and they were crossing the dance floor toward the rear exit. There was another man walking with them, older and rather distinguished-looking, Nick thought. And there was a discreet circle of bodyguards and entourage moving in a phalanx along with them.

Nick shot a look at Joyce. Obviously, she had hoped he wouldn't spot Sugai, but he had.

"You know," he told her as gently as he would have told his kids, "there's nothing stupid about being scared, but you can't just stand still and shiver. You have to choose a side."

Joyce nodded. "I did," she told him. "I'm on my side. And you're on your own."

Nick shrugged. He turned over the cards—she had twenty-one to his sixteen. "You win," he pointed out. "I guess I'm going to have to be the soft touch."

He put out his hand, but she just stood there looking as if she still didn't know what kind of guy he was. "Come on, Chicago," he said. "It's a hand. People back your way shake them."

Joyce had to smile, finally, and she took his hand. He was crude and impatient, but he had a certain charm, and maybe she'd been in Japan too long, but she found herself falling for it.

Down on the stage, the spotlight was on Charlie Vincent, who was very drunk, crooning a Ray Charles song loudly and only slightly off-key into the mike. The lyrics were traveling across the monitor screen in Japanese, but that was all right. Charlie didn't need them. With one hand he gestured suggestively, with the other he held on to an embarrassed Masahiro, who was trying to slink away.

Masahiro finally joined in on the chorus, or what should have been the chorus. But he was so intense and so out of rhythm it was impossible to tell if they were singing together or dueling with two different songs. At laughter from the drunken audience, Masahiro stopped singing, but Charlie nudged him and smiled encouragingly, and Masahiro started to belt it out.

A burst of applause and Masahiro blushed furiously, but took the bow. Charlie stepped back into the spotlight with him for the call-and-response chorus. More or less together, they whooped out the words in a final crescendo.

The crowd loved it. Masahiro loved it, Charlie loved it.

But Nick didn't even see it. He was hurrying across the floor in the direction Sugai and his entourage had taken. When he got to the rear door, his way was blocked by a hulking *sumo*—one of those super-plump wrestlers whose size is comparable only to their strength.

Nick tried reasoning with the boss over the hulk's forbidding bicep. "Mr. Sugai?" he said, fumbling for his badge. "Detective Sergeant Conklin, NYPD. Homicide." Nobody bothered to look. Sugai ignored him, and Odd Job couldn't care less. He was too busy glowering at Nick's head as if deciding where to land the first punch. "Mr. Sugai?" Nick tried again, without much hope.

He moved forward and the guard leaned away from him, just enough to push the door open a couple of inches. Sugai was just on the other side, and there was an instant of direct eye contact. Then a fat hand encircled Nick's upper arm and he was shoved back into the room.

"Hey!" Nick called out, but Sugai was gone.

"Ain't no use to cry and moan . . ." It was Charlie's voice, rapping solemnly right behind Nick. Before he had a chance to turn around and deal with his partner's drunk-and-disorderly, another rapper chimed in with a Japanese accent and not much in the way of a beat.

"Jody's got your girl and gone." It was Assistant Inspector Matsumoto Masahiro, drunk as a skunk and rapping happily, snapping his fingers with enthusiasm but no discernible rhythm.

"Ain't no use in being blue," Charlie cued him.

"Jody's got your sister, too," Masahiro responded ecstatically.

Nick turned around to look at them. Masahiro was actually grinning. Well, so was Charlie. "How many of those did you teach him?" Nick asked, shaking his head in wonder.

"Just a few of my favorites," Charlie said.

"I got a girl, her name is Grace. She drives me wild when she sits on my face," Masahiro chanted.

Charlie smiled fondly at his protégé. "Strictly lounge act," he admitted to Nick, "but if I work with him he'll be main room in no time."

"Asses and elbows, Conklin-san," Masahiro said cheerfully.

"Yeah," said Nick. "All day long." He turned to Charlie. "Pour the act into a cab," he told him.

Masahiro went peacefully, rapping all the way home.

16

*B*y now they had discovered a shortcut from the Club Miyako to the Hotel Meiji. The city was interwoven with an intricate series of shopping arcades and malls, some underground, some at street level, and some on upper floors of office buildings. Many of them connected to each other, and most were open all night as thoroughfares. The shops and restaurants and fast-food counters closed very late, but the passageways were brightly lit twenty-four hours a day.

They made their way through the narrow, winding streets of an open-air pedestrian mall that was still jumping with midnight revelers and shoppers and strollers and home-bound workers whose lives appeared to be spent more on the job than off.

Nick and Charlie turned left at the jewelry store and a sharp right at the *sushi* stand, heading for the street that would lead to their hotel.

"What'd the tab come to?" Nick asked.

"You won't believe this. Two hundred American bucks."

Nick stopped in his tracks. "Two hundred bucks for some flapping fish?"

Charlie nodded.

"What do they charge to kill it?" Nick wondered.

Charlie laughed. "We had a couple of drinks, too, I guess," he said.

"How'd you pay?"

"Courtesy of the Osaka Prefectural Police Department," Charlie told him. "I figure we was owed. So did Masa."

Nick could hardly believe what a jerk Masahiro was—not only a suit, but a guy who'd get loaded, make an asshole of himself in public, and then volunteer to pick up the check. He was no longer just a pencil jockey who could grease the wheels for them, the guy was a menace.

"I'm asking Ohashi for another cop," he told Charlie.

They came out of the pedestrian mall onto a side street that was relatively dark and quiet. It had no sidewalk. An occasional car shot past them, even some empty cabs, but they could step aside, and it was a cool and pleasant night to be walking, especially after the smoke and din of the club. Charlie hooked his coat over one shoulder.

As they approached a fork in the road, two pinpoints of light appeared first in one direction and then immediately on the horizon of the other street. In a moment they heard the motors and saw the four lights about to converge right where they stood. Four bikers joined up and slowed down to creep past

Nick and Charlie, looking them over. They were sleek new cycles, and the riders were all dressed in black. They jeered and laughed at the *gaigins,* and then they roared off and away, four abreast, owning the street.

Nick laughed. "Punks are punks everywhere," he commented. They took the left fork.

"Nick," Charlie said, "when it comes to Masahiro, I got to say that I think you're way out of line. These people are raised on all this loyalty—*giri*—stuff."

"And I was raised on boiled potatoes," Nick said bitterly. "He almost cost us the case."

"Loyalty always costs," Charlie persisted. "You've backed up guys when it would have been easier to walk . . . like this Internal Affairs situation of yours."

It was the first time he had come right out with the sensitive subject. Nick was surprised. "What about it?" Let Charlie spill what was on his mind, maybe it was time to get it all out.

"They did come to me," Charlie told him. "More than once. But I told them where and at what angle to shove it. I don't know what you did or didn't do, Nick. I don't know and I don't care."

There was only the sound of their footsteps echoing on the lonely dark street. A black Subaru sedan came weaving past them, leaving a fading trail of male voices arguing excitedly. Then it was quiet again. Their hotel loomed up at the end of the block.

"Thanks" was all Nick managed to get out. Even he didn't know whether he meant it sincerely or sardonically.

Another blast of hot noise rose up behind them— another bike. They stepped to the side of the street, straddling the open sewer, to let it pass.

"Fuck you, too," Charlie said. "The point is, you can trust me. Because I've got standards. Just like Masahiro."

Nick stopped in his tracks and stared at Charlie. With a thunderous blast a motorcycle zoomed up from behind them. As it passed, dangerously close, the rider reached out and snatched Charlie's coat off his shoulder. The rider whooped with laughter and stormed on past.

"Motherfucker," Charlie swore. He took off after the bikes, running flat-out, on instinct.

"Fabulous," Nick muttered. Action at last, but, of course, it would be futile. He sprinted after Charlie.

The bike turned onto another street mall and suddenly there were lights again and crowds of people. Ducking and weaving, Charlie was thirty yards behind the biker who waved the coat in the air as he swung his way expertly through the narrow arcades.

"It's only a coat!" Nick yelled. "Come on, Charlie!"

"He's got my passport!" Charlie shouted as he sprinted past two unsurprised women with babies asleep on their backs. He dodged a drunken office worker who was weaving on unsteady feet toward the subway entrance.

Nick lost sight of him.

"Hey, Charlie! Charlie!"

There was an escalator going down just where he had last spotted Charlie—using his partner-sense, Nick took the moving stairs down five at a clip. It was an underground parking garage, vast and dark and smelling of grease and danger.

"Charlie!"

Charlie was there, all right. He had spotted the biker, too.

"Drop it!" he called out in the cavernous depths of the garage. Nick heard him and edged cautiously in Charlie's direction.

The biker had stopped and was looking back at Charlie. His black helmet reflected no light at all. He held Charlie's coat up high and let it drop to the cement floor. He revved up his engine and cruised twenty or so yards away. He stopped and looked back at Charlie, waiting.

Charlie walked over and picked up his coat.

"Come here, amigo," he challenged the biker.

Coat in hand, he walked slowly toward the black-clad figure on the sleek black machine. "Over here, Nicky!" he called out as he approached the bike. "Come on, friend," he said quietly to the biker, "you gonna run off again?"

The bike thrummed but its rider didn't move a muscle.

"Or are we gonna have a little chat now?" Charlie continued. Nick was about fifty yards behind him now.

With an ear-splitting howl, three more bikes appeared from three different corridors of the vast underground maze. Charlie spun around as the bikers streaked past him from all directions. They taunted him, passing close enough to reach out and prick him with the steel that glinted in their hands.

They spun around, sticking it to him over and over, and then suddenly they *varooomed* away through the pockets of light and dark into the recesses of the garage. Charlie, grabbing his stomach, staggered a step or two. Blood poured out from between his hands. He stared down at it.

"Jesus Christ," he whispered.

"Charlie!" Nick shouted, sprinting toward him.

He was too late. The biker got there first. He had thrown off his helmet/mask, and even as he ran toward Charlie, Nick recognized Sato.

Charlie stumbled backward, still on his feet but barely. Sato and his bike made one final pass before Nick could get to Charlie. Screeching a guttural yell, Sato charged in, holding up the gleaming blade of his *tanto*.

"Charlie!" Nick yelled. He had never felt so helpless in his life.

With one whack of his sword at a speed of seventy-five miles per hour, Sato decapitated Charlie Vincent in front of Nick Conklin's horrified, unbelieving eyes.

"NOOOOOO!" Nick screamed. He ran toward Sato, who had stopped his bike to gloat. Sato looked back at Nick, and then he made a cutting motion with his finger above his eyebrow and sped away, his three pals right behind him.

"SATO!"

Nick's voice echoed in the empty garage, ricocheting through the corridors and tunnels and coming back to him as the sounds of the bikes faded in the distance. He ran to Charlie and fell to his knees. For one crazy moment he thought he could cradle Charlie's poor bloody head and put it back on his grotesquely severed neck. But the two hideous wet mops of flesh had nothing to do with the bright, witty, quick, and honest partner of a moment ago. Charlie, was gone. He was dead and this apparition was some vile nightmare spewing out its thick crimson ooze onto the greasy cold floor. It had nothing to do with Charlie Vincent. That good man was gone. Charlie was dead and a minute ago he had been alive, and there wasn't a goddamned thing Nick Conklin could do to bring him back.

17

*N*ick's head was in some kind of echo chamber. It was filled with insulating material and he was in the depths of a profound silence that cut him away from everything else in the world but his own shock and grief. His blood was boiling with pain and isolation and loss and an escalating anger fiercer than he had ever experienced before. He heard nothing for a long time, not even his own shallow breathing, and then—maybe a minute, maybe a year later—he became dimly aware of voices shouting meaningless words. Someone was pulling at his sleeve, wanting him to stand up, to leave Charlie all alone on that garage floor on the other side of the world, far from home.

They were jabbering in Japanese. Cops. Lots of Jap cops wanting Nick to talk, tell them what happened.

An ambulance and paramedics hovered around. Someone was being sick at the sight of Charlie's head rolled away from the rest of him. Police photographers and crowd-controllers with cameras and barricades and chalk to mark the spot.

"You must tell us what happened," one of the cops finally said in English.

Slowly, the feeling came back in Nick's body, and he saw that he still had arms and hands and feet and legs and all these things could move, and he stood up. Ignoring the cops and paramedics and the crowd, he walked out of the garage through one of the long corridors into the neon night. No one tried to stop him. They knew who he was and where they could find him.

Funny, it had been so mild only a few minutes ago that Charlie had slung his coat over his shoulder instead of wearing it, but now the air was chilling and the wind was bitter.

Nick didn't know where he was walking—or care. The streets were still bustling with people going places, buying things, staggering with drink and laughing. Laughing . . . as if life was the same as it had been an hour ago.

He was walking across a bridge. A toothless, wizened beggar held a hand out to him, mumbling pathetically. Nick looked into the aged face and wondered why this man was still trying to stay alive. He dug into his pocket and came up with a handful of yen for the old man, who blessed him or cursed him—it didn't matter which. Nick leaned against the railing of the bridge and stared down at the water below. Cars raced past him and people hurried by, huddled against the wind.

A car stopped. Its door slammed. High heels clattered on the pavement, coming toward him.

"Nick?"

He didn't turn around. He barely heard, didn't care.

"Come on, Nick," she said again, linking her arm through his. She turned him around, and he let her lead him to the car, into the passenger seat. She went around and got behind the wheel.

He didn't look at her. He didn't see Masahiro, who had gotten out of the car and now stood a few feet away, holding his briefcase, giving Joyce the nod. Nick didn't see anything except Charlie, running and wisecracking and being brave, and lying on a garage floor with his body in one place and his head somewhere else.

Joyce took him to her apartment. He went quietly, still in silent shock and allowing himself to be led. It was a modern high-rise building, and her place was quiet and serene, more East than West. A comfortable couch faced the wide windows with the lights of Osaka forming a gaudy mural below. She made him a stiff drink and led him to the couch. He sank down on the *tatami* mat that covered the floor, leaning his head back against the couch, looking out at the view, seeing only Charlie.

Joyce was wearing her working clothes—sexy silk form-fitting dress and her masses of soft blond hair piled high on her head, a couple of chunks of glimmering jewels in her ears. Not that Nick noticed. She fixed her own drink and sat down on the couch, within reach but far enough to give him room.

After the first jolt, Nick put his brandy down. He stared out at the lights and darkness. Joyce waited, wise enough to say nothing. After a long while he started to talk.

"He should have known better. He was raised in the city."

His voice cracked; he was close to tears. Let them come, she hoped silently, you'll feel a lot better if you can let it out.

"My job . . ." Nick said, "in my job you see the endings—the way things are."

She waited.

"You don't have to see people whole one minute and then—" He choked and wasn't sure he was going to be in control for very long. "He was twenty-eight fucking years old!" It came out in a terrible, ache-filled wail, and then searing tears were pouring down his cheeks and he didn't try to stop them or wipe them away, and she moved closer so that she could be there if he needed her.

When he came back to the world, he was on the couch, covered with a quilt. Outside the window, the sky was clear bright blue now. The buildings of Osaka looked closer and less mysterious in daylight. A huge carp-shaped kite, gaily colored and trailing a long tail, drifted across his view. At the same moment, he was conscious of the almost unbearably sad-sweet tenor saxophone of Charlie Parker blowing the blues.

The song ended and a snappy radio voice said, "That was Bird, from the Blue Note years. Zero nine-forty hours and fifty-two degrees in central Osaka. This is specialist Doug Dale bringing you 'Tapestries in Jazz' on the Far East Network, Armed Forces Radio . . . and now . . ."

Nick got to his feet. He was feeling stiff and trying not to think of the way Charlie had looked the last time he saw him. He looked around the room.

It was the most Japanese room he had seen since landing in Japan. *Tatami* mats on the floor, sparse furnishings, and everything squared away and neat as a pin. There was a shelf with some photos on it, mostly of Joyce herself. He looked at each one carefully. There she was at a baseball game surrounded by grinning Japanese businessmen in suits and ties. There was one of her at the Club Miyako, looking gorgeously decked out for some special occasion. At about age twenty, she had her hair dyed dark, long eyelashes, and a miniskirt. Even younger, there she was hugging a huge sheep dog on a suburban lawn. There were pictures of family, too—the regulation mom and dad and a few friends or siblings.

"Did you get any sleep?"

He turned to see Joyce standing in the doorway, wearing a simple skirt and cotton blouse, clutching a bag of groceries. She wasn't wearing any makeup, and her hair was down, combed and parted neatly, falling to her shoulders. She looked like the younger sister of the woman he knew from the Club Miyako.

"Not much," he said.

"What are you looking at?" It was not an unfriendly question, just a curious one. She was smiling and she looked terribly sweet and nice and even vulnerable, and he felt very grateful to her.

"Your photos," he said. "I like the one with the dog."

She laughed and set the groceries down on a low table.

And suddenly neither of them seemed to be able to think of anything to say. It was a little awkward—two people who had shared something intimate but didn't know each other at all.

"What's the dog's name?" Nick asked.

"Alma."

"Mine was Spot," he told her, and for some reason, that broke the ice and they both instantly fell at ease and it was all right.

"Do you like Canadian bacon?" she asked, heading for the little efficiency kitchen.

"Love it," he said. He followed her. "Can I help?"

"You know how to make coffee?"

"Sure."

"You can help."

They ate breakfast, sitting on the floor, because there were no chairs for dining. Joyce sat very comfortably on her haunches in the Japanese style, but Nick didn't know what to do with his legs under the low table. He tried the haunch method, but his muscles rebelled at the unaccustomed strain, and so he made the best of it by changing position a lot. But the American-style breakfast was perfect—fresh-squeezed orange juice, crisp bacon, and eggs over-easy, with lots of freshly ground coffee.

"I forgot what food tasted like," Nick told her. "Thanks."

"I know. It takes a while to get used to the local cuisine," she agreed. "More coffee?"

He held out his cup and she poured for him. "I don't get it," he told her frankly. "You . . . all of this . . ." He gestured around the room and at the city outside.

Joyce nodded. "You mean what's a nice girl like me doing in a place like this?" she said, grinning. "Well . . . blondes are a big commodity here. I pull in more every week than I did tending bar for a month in Chicago. For the first time in my whole life, I've got something going." She laughed. "They think I'm exotic—how about that?"

Well, he kind of thought so, too, and he knew lots of blondes, but he didn't tell her that.

"How about you?" she asked him. "You got family?"

"An ex-wife, couple of kids," he said.

Joyce got serious all of a sudden. "Do them a favor," she said. "Go home."

Before he could say anything, someone knocked on the door of the apartment.

"Are you expecting anyone?" Nick asked her.

"I wasn't expecting you," she said as she got gracefully to her feet. She went to the door and looked through the peephole, then opened it to admit Masahiro.

He was dressed in his best black suit and black tie. He was holding two parcels.

Nick didn't know what the hell was going on, but it only took him a minute to realize that Masahiro must have sicked Joyce onto him in the first place, a rescue operation. He had been too out of it the night before to wonder at her finding him in the middle of the neon jungle. Masahiro must have sent her. Now here he was, ludicrously holding a formally wrapped gift and a plain cardboard box.

Masahiro and Joyce began some kind of weird bowing routine while Nick watched, mystified. Masahiro bowed to Joyce. Joyce returned the bow. He said something, she said something, they bowed again. He handed her the gift and she accepted with a slightly different kind of bow and a few words. Then she turned and explained briefly to Nick. "He has come on a formal condolence call. It is a custom to bring a gift." She went into the kitchen.

Masahiro came to the table where Nick was trying to unpretzel his legs. He sat down across from Nick and set the plain cardboard box squarely on the table. He sat on his haunches with his back rigid and straight as a board.

"I am very sorry for your loss," he said solemnly. "I thought you should know—I made all the arrangements for Charlie."

Nick nodded. "That was good of you," he said. "I appreciate it."

"I feel . . ." Masa was uncharacteristically fumbling for words. Joyce came out of the kitchen with a teapot and cups, set them in front of Masahiro with a slight bow, and then retired to the bedroom without a word.

"I feel that had I been with you, perhaps it would not have come to this . . ." Masahiro said. He bowed deeply to Nick. "I'm very sorry," he said.

Nick could only nod. That big lump was coming into his throat again and he didn't trust himself to say anything.

Masahiro moved the cardboard box an inch or two closer to Nick. "These are his things," he said quietly. "We have a tradition. When we . . . when someone close to us dies, we keep something personal of theirs."

Masahiro seemed to want Nick to open the box, but he couldn't, not now. He didn't touch it or even look at it. Whatever was inside was all that was left of Charlie.

"Maybe later," he said. His voice sounded hollow inside the huge cavernous isolation that had descended again.

"Please," Masahiro insisted quietly.

Nick looked at him. There was something in the way the assistant inspector said that which cut through the sadness and pain and told Nick to listen. Almost of their own volition, his hands reached out to the box. He took off the lid and looked inside.

There were the odds and ends of Charlie Vincent's life: passport, wallet, keys, the map of Osaka . . . There was Charlie's Zippo lighter, with the NYPD crest on it. Nick picked it up, held it in his palm, then dropped it into his pocket. All right, this he would keep. He touched Charlie's comb and his little black notebook. There wasn't a whole lot there. The guidebook to Japan seemed to be at the bottom, but when Nick picked it up he got a surprise. Under the guidebook was Charlie's .32 Beretta and an extra clip.

Nick didn't touch the gun. He looked up at Masahiro, eyed him carefully, trying to figure it.

"Can I take what I want?" he asked.

Masahiro had anticipated the question. Holding Nick's gaze, he replied evenly, "Anything." Then he said, "Until the day I die I will be in your debt."

Nick reached into his pocket and withdrew Charlie's lighter. He rubbed the crest and then held it out across the table for Masahiro to take. "He was your friend, too," he said.

Masahiro bowed and accepted the gift. Then Nick reached into the box and took the Beretta and the clip and stashed it in his inside pocket.

"I want to go back to Sato's hideout," he told Masahiro. "Just you and me."

Masahiro sat silently, showing no reaction.

"Are you with me?" Nick pressed him.

After a pause, Masahiro nodded.

"Let's go, then."

Nick got up awkwardly from the floor, shook his deadwood legs until they tingled and seemed relatively serviceable again, and knocked on the bedroom door. Joyce opened it, and all she had to do was look at him and Masahiro to figure out the next move. They were heading someplace Masahiro didn't think was healthy, but they were in it together.

She smiled up at Nick and he leaned over to kiss her. It was a sweet kiss, tender and friendly.

"Thanks," he said.

"Take care, Nick," she told him.

He stared at her, startled. Nobody had said those words to him in a long, long time.

18

*T*he pachinko parlor was crowded with morning players. Every machine was in action, and the clink of hundreds of thousands of tiny steel balls spewing up and cascading down the vertical traps and tunnels sounded like the assembly line in a ball-bearing plant. Every player seemed to have at least one kibitzer—a friend, husband, wife, schoolmate, grandpa, or maybe just a baby peering over its mother's shoulder at the noisy, colorful, hypnotic action.

Nick and Masahiro worked their way through the narrow aisles full of players and watchers and people waiting their turns. Nick led the way to the rear stairs and went straight on up. The door at the top had not been repaired, but replaced with a board held in place with randomly crossed two-by-fours.

Rage and grief gave him strength. Nick ripped the two-by-fours off and kicked in the temporary partition. The room was dark, all the shades drawn and lights out. He felt for a wall switch but didn't find any. Masahiro felt his way to the center of the room and found a string hanging down, pulled on the bare bulb that swung back and forth casting a crazy light over the remains of the once cozy, now chaotic, room. Everything had been thoroughly picked over.

Masahiro swung the ruins of the door back into place behind them. Nick stood in the middle of the room and looked around at the abandoned mess.

"What did your people find?" he asked Masahiro.

"Stolen police uniforms . . . Sato's clothes . . . Kleenex with lipstick . . ."

"Prints?"

Masahiro nodded. "Sato's. And those of two known criminals. There were others, not able to be identified."

Nick cast a long, slow look around. Everything was upended and pushed or pulled out of place—chairs and couches away from the walls, rugs pulled up, drawers hanging open with their contents jumbled. He felt the heat of being close, but not close enough.

"Son of a bitch was here," he muttered. He went over to the desk and ripped a drawer out, letting it crash upside down onto the floor. Just for the hell of it, he put his foot through the bottom of the drawer. He went over to the doorway leading to the bedroom and pulled up the mattress of the bed, examining the springs and slats with one disgusted look. "He slept here . . . ate here . . . screwed here . . . had himself a little party . . ."

He came back to the main room and was pleased to see Masahiro rifling through a cabinet. He turned back to take the bedroom apart, starting with a hamper which he dumped on the floor. He sifted through every piece of dirty clothing and then examined the hamper itself for hidden spaces. He ripped the quilt from the bed, let the feathers and down fly everywhere while he deftly fingered every inch of it for suspicious lumps or crinkles. Nothing in the closet escaped his eye, and when he was finished with the drawers and chair cushions and pillows and window frames, he began methodically to peel away the wallpaper.

In the cooking area, they dumped food containers and sifted through the mess with careful fingers. Masahiro smelled the tea and Nick ran it through a sieve. Shelf paper was suspect, sugar and salt and cinnamon and soy sauce—nothing escaped their assiduous attention.

In the bathroom, Nick removed the drain stopper from the sink and bathtub and pulled out the thick goo that had accumulated there. Cleaning his fingers carefully in newspaper, he found he had come up with a mess of black hair.

They had different techniques. Nick was rough but thorough. Masahiro handled even the toughest objects as if they were glass. But finally the job got done. Not an atom in that apartment had gone unsearched, no ordinary surface had been taken for granted, and nothing had been found. It was hours before they stopped, exhausted and scoreless.

"He felt so safe," Nick muttered. "So fucking safe." Nick closed his eyes and leaned against the ripped-open wall. "I'm still here, you bastard!" he shouted.

When he opened his eyes they fell onto a soiled *futon* that he had ripped open and eviscerated hours before. Something caught his eye—a glitter. He moved over to it and looked very closely. It was just a sequin. He had seen it before and it didn't register. Now maybe it did. He stared at it for a minute.

"Nick, there is nothing more here. I think we should—"

Nick touched his hand to the sequins. They stuck to his damp palm.

"Masa, looky here." He held out his hand.

Masahiro looked. "Yes. Sequins. From a lady's dress, I would assume."

"What lady?"

Masahiro shrugged, failing to get the drift. "Could be any lady. Sequins are very popular with a certain kind of lady."

"Black and white," Nick noted. "There's a hostess at the Miyako who's got a black-and-white sequin dress, and guess what? I saw her with Sato last night."

"Sato has many women."

"This one also had blood on her sequins the night before."

"Yes. Our men have questioned her. There is nothing more to learn from her," Masahiro said.

"We could follow her. She works at the club, and where does she go after work? Maybe to visit her pal Sato, huh?"

"You saw them together only once?" Masahiro pointed out, tactful but dubious.

"Yeah, at the club last night. But she's been here, too. These sequins came off her ass."

"Perhaps. Perhaps some other lady's ass." Masahiro sighed.

"You got a better idea?"

Masahiro looked thoughtful. "No, Nick."

"Then let's go."

They were surprised to find that it was dark outside.

"Will you allow me to treat you to a *teriyaki* dinner?" Masahiro asked, almost shyly.

"I'll tell you what—let's go to McDonald's. My treat," Nick countered.

Masahiro nodded thoughtfully. "You do not trust me to order food for you. I don't blame you."

"Oh, hell, you want *teriyaki,* we'll get *teriyaki.* What the hell, I'll give it a try," Nick said.

"This time I take you to a very tasty place."

"You're on," Nick agreed. He didn't know whether he was mellowing toward this guy on account of Charlie, or whether he just didn't give a damn what he ate anymore—also because of Charlie.

Masahiro was as good as his word. He drove to a quieter district, and they went into a restaurant. Delicious scents wafted from the kitchen. They were treated with great honor by the owner and served elegantly. The meat and chicken were succulent and the sauce was tasty and rich. The owner even produced a fork for Nick.

When they left, the owner bowed to them and Masahiro bowed back, and then they did it again. Nick waited till it was all over then held out his hand to shake the owner's hand and said, "Goodbye." Turning to Masahiro he said, "Tell him it was delicious."

Masahiro smiled and delivered the message along with another series of bows and *sayonaras.* When they got outside, it had started to rain. They drove in Masahiro's old Toyota to the Club Miyako and sat in the rain, cramped but cozy, until closing time. The car was not only old but also small, and Nick's knees were up around his ears the whole time.

Taxis began rolling up to the curb and forming a line, waiting for customers. The doorman stood between the awning and the curb, holding an umbrella over clients and girls as they climbed into the cabs. Norie came out with a party of drunks, arm in arm in arm. Her giggles could be heard down the block. Nick and Masahiro sat peering through the rain at the doorway.

"That's her," Nick said suddenly. The sequin dress had been changed for a silk one, but it was the same young woman. She came out of the club with two other hostesses and they stood under the awning for a moment, saying goodnight.

Masahiro turned the key and started the cranky engine. It balked, coughed, turned over and purred, with an occasional hiccup. They waited.

"That's right, night-night, bye-bye . . ." Nick said impatiently, his eyes on the girl. "Okay, put it in the taxi, sweetheart, and take me to your leader."

She finally got into the waiting taxi and it pulled away from the curb. The rain cut visibility so much they had to trail a lot closer than was comfortable, and the cab was making reckless time. Even though Masahiro was driving cautiously and deliberately, the creaky little Toyota tended to spin out when they took the rain-slick corners. They fell behind, and it got harder to keep the taxi in sight through the teeming downpour and jangle of late-night traffic.

"Move," Nick urged. "You're losing her. Kiss her chrome."

Masahiro made a hissing sound between his teeth — concentration and, apparently, agreement. He put his foot down on the gas. But he said, "How can you be so sure? It could be any girl's dress, Nick, you know that. If you ask me, this is a wild-turkey chase."

"Goose," Nick said. "Look, sometimes you have to forget your head and lead with your balls."

Masahiro was thinking this over and automatically slowing for a yellow-turning-red light. "Go, go!" Nick urged him. "Through the light. Go!"

The assistant inspector put his foot to the floor and tore through the intersection. Astonished drivers coming from all directions screeched up short and honked as they hit their brakes. It was against all the rules! But Masahiro was clearly pleased with himself; for once, his face revealed his feelings: the desk man was excited and exhilarated by his own daring.

"Balls," Nick heard him mutter under his breath, repeating the lesson so he would be sure to remember. They didn't lose the cab again. There were a couple of turns that the old clunker took on two skidding wheels, but they stayed with it, out of the pleasure district onto a wide elegant boulevard and down a quiet residential street where the houses were set back and separated from each other by wide lawns, manicured trees, and high walls.

The cab pulled into the circular driveway of a spectacular house in the traditional Japanese style— huge but simple lines, with opaque *shoji* screens letting in the light and keeping out the world.

Masahiro stopped the car a few yards back from the entrance to the driveway. He didn't turn off the engine. Nick peered up at the mansion looming up in the chiaroscuro of the occasional bolts of lightning against the blackness of the night.

"Sato's in there," Nick said quietly. He felt the

adrenaline rising in his blood and coursing through his body. He was sure.

"If he is," Masahiro said, "he is already dead."

"What?! What are you talking about?" Nick shot back.

"This is Sugai's house," Masahiro told him.

Nick's eyes went wide, but the instant he had digested this information he nodded excitedly. "No shit," he said thoughtfully. "Well, now . . . this girl is screwing everybody but Santa in the Macy's Thanksgiving Day Parade. It's perfect."

Masahiro put it together quickly. "Sato's eyes and ears?"

Nick nodded.

Masahiro smiled. "Fabulous," he said. He settled back for another long wait. Nick shifted around in the cramped seat in his futile search for a comfortable position. The windows were fogged on the inside, dripping on the outside, and the car was full of the cigarette smoke of the last few hours, with more hours to come.

19

There was no traffic in this street at this hour—the top executives who lived in these homes no longer had to play the game of drunken camaraderie with their colleagues; they had risen to the top and had earned their sleep. The thick hedges and walls and lines of perfectly trimmed trees guaranteed quiet for the privileged in their mansions. It also meant that no one was likely to hear a car that waited outside on the street.

"Music?" Masahiro suggested. At Nick's raised eyebrows, he reached into the back seat for his briefcase. He snapped it open and showed Nick the stash of cassette tapes neatly stacked inside.

"Japanese bagpipes? No, thanks," Nick said.

Masahiro smiled. He pulled out a tape and inserted it in the radio cassette player. In a second—Sam Cooke's "You Send Me."

"Saint Sam!" Nick exclaimed. "Masa, you are full

of surprises." Idly, he peered into the briefcase that lay open on Masahiro's lap. Besides the cassettes, there was a .38 pistol, snapped into its holster, a matched set of walkie-talkies, and a clean shirt.

"This could come in handy," he said, taking one of the walkie-talkies and shoving it into the pocket of his jacket. Then he pointed to the gun. "No one's going to give you time to dig that thing out of there," he told Masahiro.

"In twenty-eight years I've never had to use it," Masahiro said. "You?"

"I work homicide in South Brooklyn," Nick said. "Even the nuns carry guns."

Masahiro was incredulous. "Have you shot many people?" he asked.

Nick shook his head. "I only shot back," he retorted.

"What happened?"

Nick shrugged. "They missed." He shifted his position. Masahiro started to snap the briefcase shut but Nick held out his hand to stop him. "Do me a favor," he asked. "Strap it on."

Masahiro looked startled.

"We're not working files and records," Nick pointed out, not unkindly.

Masahiro took out the holster and clipped it to his belt. "You know, Nick, I've been in some tough spots before," he said.

"Oh?"

"Oh, yes. I worked security during Marilyn Monroe's visit with DiMaggio-san. Very demanding."

Nick twisted in his seat. He was interested. "Oh, yeah? What was she like?" he asked.

"Oh . . . blond." Masahiro floundered helplessly.

"Very sexy," he assured Nick. Then he broke down, ashamed of his exaggerated claim. "Actually, I just kept the crowds back. Not so tough, really . . ."

"Oh, well, crowds can get ugly sometimes," Nick assured him.

They sat in silence for a few minutes listening to Sam Cooke. Then Masahiro said softly, "It's been an interesting few days, Nick."

Before Nick could respond, they saw lights coming from Sugai's gate. A sleek dark limo glided out of the driveway. Nick nudged Masahiro with his elbow. "Home, James," he said.

The limo snaked like a reptile in its element along the shining wet streets, heading for the freeway. The clunky old Toyota sedan kept up with it just fine. Masahiro had tossed away his customary caution somewhere in the night, and it was obvious to Nick that the assistant inspector was in fact enjoying the chase. When they turned up the ramp onto the freeway the speed doubled and Masahiro had his foot on the floor and a grin on his face.

Nick was trying to dope out the situation. Three in the morning she arrives in a taxi, an hour later the limo rolls out—odds are, with her in it. Now where? Home to Sato? Maybe. Maybe not.

"That's a nice limo," Nick commented. "Maybe he's sending her to somebody for his birthday."

"Traditionally, Japanese don't celebrate birthdays," Masahiro told him. The windshield wipers were whooshing wildly back-and-forth but not shaving close enough to keep the vision clear without straining.

"You could see the downside of a blowjob, Masa," Nick told him. "Just drive."

Masahiro thought that one over as he concentrated on driving. The limousine turned off the ramp near the waterfront, and the Toyota skidded wildly but righted itself about a quarter of an inch before it hit the railing. Masahiro kept his foot on the gas, though, and never lost sight of the quarry. The limo slowed to cruise the fish-market area, which was in the throes of its early-morning activities. Fishermen and wholesalers were delivering baskets and barrels of live squirming catch, shouting deals like the floor of the world's busiest stock-market exchange. The ground was awash with rain and fish scales and a few dead fish that got away. The limo slowed to a stop and the beautiful young hostess stepped out.

Before Masahiro could brake on the slippery pavement, Nick threw open the door and bailed out. He hurried after the girl, who had made her way between two stalls into the maze of the market.

"Let's keep in touch," he muttered, grabbing the walkie-talkie as he ran. "Masa, you read me?"

"Yes, Nick."

"She's stopped at one of the stalls, talking with an old man. They know each other."

"I do not think Sato would disguise himself as a fishmonger," Masahiro said. "Perhaps it means that she comes this way often."

"He's offering her a fish. Yuck."

"Is she taking it?"

"Wait a minute. No. Not today. She's thanking him prettily and—okay, here we go. She's on her way, and me, too."

The young woman worked her way through a sea of workers who were bathed in steam from dry ice. Nick stayed reasonably close—it did dawn on him that Masahiro would have been less conspicuous, but he was staying low, and the market was teeming with people buying and selling and haggling, and fish flopping and squirming. There were even some tourists watching and taking pictures. No one was paying much attention to the tall sandy-haired middle-aged American in blue jeans and leather jacket who sauntered in and out of the stalls and around the pillars with his hands in his pockets.

The girl left the market and crossed a street and went into an apartment building. It was neither an elegant building nor was it run-down. A sleepy doorman answered her ring and let her in. After a couple of minutes, a light went on in a third-floor window.

Nick pulled out the walkie-talkie. "Okay, Masa, come in."

"I'm here, Nick."

"I got her. I'm on the other side of the market. She's gone into a building across the street. Why don't you bring the wheels around here?"

"Okay, be right there."

He had to drive all around the perimeter of the fish market, but Masahiro was getting his wings as a daredevil now and made it in just a couple of minutes, whooshing up in a puddle of rainwater right near where Nick was standing. He waited but Nick refused to coil himself back up into that sardine can for another endless wait. He motioned to Masahiro to get out, and pointed to a *soba* stand nearby. Masahiro was quick to jump out, lock the car, and follow him to the warm, dry, brightly lit café.

They sat where they could keep an eye on the third-floor window of the building across the street. Once, they saw her silhouette pass behind the shade.

The *soba* stand was large, immaculately clean with white tile floors and constantly swabbed Formica counters. There were many customers, all shoveling in the soft noodles with chopsticks, the bowls held close to their mouths. The sound of satisfied slurping must have pleased the aged proprietress. She handed out bowl after bowl and smiled and nodded cheerfully despite her lack of front teeth.

Masahiro ordered for both of them. "You like *soba?*" he asked Nick.

Nick shrugged. "I never managed to get any in my mouth. Charlie was starting to get the hang of it, though."

"Shall I show you how to hold the chopsticks, then?"

"Yeah, okay."

Patiently, Masahiro placed the sticks in Nick's hand and showed him how to use the lower one for balance, the upper one doing all the moving. Then the proprietress brought their warm steaming bowls of noodles to them and stood watching and waiting to see how Nick would do.

"You want some pepper?" Masahiro offered.

"Ah, yeah, please." Nick sprinkled the hot stuff liberally.

Masahiro took a deep slurp. "Good, huh?" He beamed.

Nick held the chopsticks the way he had just been shown. The aged woman shyly reached to correct the angle, and then she beamed encouragement at him. He lifted the bowl with his other hand. The old woman nodded again, and Nick tried scooping the noodles into his mouth with the sticks the way everyone else was doing. The slippery stuff slid right off the sticks, some back into the bowl, some onto the table. The old woman wiped up the spill with her towel and then, meekly at first, she took Nick's hand in her own and showed him how to do it. He concentrated. Across the table, Masahiro smiled encouragingly. The old woman nodded and Nick went for it. He got the noodles almost to his mouth before they dropped again.

The woman laughed. So did Nick.

She said something in Japanese and he knew exactly what she was saying: "This is how you hold the chopsticks, try again."

"Thank you," he told her. And then, almost shyly, he said it in her language: *"Domo arigato."*

Masahiro grinned happily. "Big shot from New York," he said.

With the old woman's encouragement, Nick tried again and then again, and he got a mouthful at last and then another, and suddenly he had the hang of it and no problem. He even started making slurping noises. They sort of came out by themselves. The old woman beamed with pride and went to the bar. She came back with two chilled beers, which she set down in front of them. Then she left them alone.

"Nick-san," Masahiro said hesitantly. "There is something . . . maybe I shouldn't ask."

"What?" Nick said, shoveling in the delicious *soba*, washing it down with a sip of beer. "You can ask me anything you want, it's okay. What do you want to know?"

Masahiro took a sip of beer, too. Then he said, "These things . . . disturbing things, that I hear about you in New York . . ."

Nick nodded. "A couple of guys I used to work with in the department took some money from some drug dealers," he said flatly.

"They stole?" Masahiro was shocked.

Nick shrugged. "They liberated funds," he said.

"Theft is theft," Masahiro said firmly. "There is no gray area."

"Listen, Masa, New York is one big goddamned gray area. The bums went to the joint. It's not like anybody got hurt."

"It dishonors all policemen," Masahiro insisted. He watched Nick spearing the last of the noodles in the bowl, only dropping about one out of three mouthfuls now. After a beat, he asked, "Did you take money, Nick?"

Nick set the bowl down. He looked across the counter at his partner. Somehow he knew there was no point in lying to Masahiro.

"Yeah," he said finally. "I took money. I'm not proud of it. Okay, you know I got a divorce. I got kids and I got bills. There's no way out."

He felt like shit but he was glad he had leveled. Masahiro regarded him with no change in his expression. "Did Charlie know?" he asked.

Nick didn't have to answer.

"He was a policeman, Nick," Masahiro went on. "If you steal, you disgrace him. Whether he is dead or alive. And yourself. And me."

Nick looked him in the eye. The two men sat silently facing each other. Nick wanted to laugh it off, but he couldn't. He took a sip of beer. When he put the glass down, Masahiro refilled it for him. Nick offered Masahiro a cigarette; they each took one and Masahiro lit them both from his Zippo with the NYPD crest.

20

*N*ick stood watch while Masahiro checked out the name on the mailbox for the third-floor front apartment. The rain had slowed to a freezing drizzle and daylight was lighting up the sky on the other side of the river. When Masahiro came hurrying back, his collar was turned up and his hair was slicked down over his forehead like wet licorice.

"Must be her own place. Just one name—Miyuki Haroshi."

"That's a girl's name?" Nick double-checked.

"Female, yes."

Before he could get a cultural lecture on patronymics in Japanese tradition, Nick hustled Masahiro over to the car and they climbed inside.

"Might as well grab some sleep if you can," he told Masahiro.

"Oh, no, you first, Nick. Please."

"Are you kidding? I can't even find a way to sit comfortably in this kiddie-car, much less stretch out for a nap. No, anyway, I'm not tired. Grab forty, Masa, I'll watch for Miyuki."

Masahiro understood the wisdom of this. He nodded, pulled out a clean white handkerchief and laid it over his face, then put his head back and almost instantly began to snore. Nick watched the daylight change the fish market and the street from early-morning bustle to rush hour for the working stiffs. Salarymen and women began to stir in the windows of the apartment buildings; lights went on, then shades went up, and when the sun had fully risen, the lights went off again. People began trickling and then pouring out of the buildings on their way to work. Nick tried doing some aerobic exercises, but there wasn't even room for a neck stretch without bumping his head on the roof. Both of his feet were asleep and he was getting sick of the view.

And then she came out of her building—a gorgeous dream in designer silks—sleekly fitted black silk slacks and a matching tailored jacket. Nick poked Masahiro, who woke instantly. They stared at her as she hailed a cab. By the time she stepped into it, Masahiro had the old Toyota warm and ready.

"Very nice, isn't she?" Nick commented. "Not a sequin in sight. She must be on her way to morning Mass."

They took off after her.

The cab led them across the river, along the quay, and into an elegant shopping district. It pulled up in front of a department store featuring French clothing, English silver, and Russian caviar in its windows. Miyuki paid the driver and went inside the store.

There was no standing or parking anywhere on this street. "I'll go with her, Masa," Nick said. "Park the car as fast as you can and find me in there. We'll take turns so she doesn't get wise." He jumped out of the car and went inside the posh store, unconsciously smoothing his hair back, suddenly aware of his height and his New York Sloppy style. Everyone in the place looked as band-box as Miyuki. He played dumb-ass tourist and stayed as far behind her as he dared. He just prayed he wasn't going to have to lurk around any goddamned lingerie department.

Up the escalator, a floor behind, keeping his eye on her without appearing to, he trailed her to the third floor, where she began talking to a saleswoman beautiful enough to be a model. After a few minutes, she sat down on an upholstered settee, and Nick settled behind a kind of pillar where he could look like he was waiting for a wife, he hoped. The saleswoman turned out to be a model after all—she came out in a different dress—a gown, really, Nick supposed—and walked slowly, turning and turning so Miyuki could examine it closely. A little more conversation and the model disappeared to come out in a moment in a different outfit. Nick yawned.

Nick heard loud breathing beside him and looked up—there was Masahiro, who'd obviously run all the way back from where he'd parked the car. "The car is in the garage of this building, two hundred yen per hour. I don't even know if I can get reimbursed—we still don't know if this is the girl who can take us to—" Masahiro was huffing and puffing from his efforts.

"That whole car isn't worth two hundred yen, is it?"

Nick asked. "I'll be just down the street, watching for her to come out the door. Signal me whether to pick up the tail or let you carry the ball, okay?"

"Okay," Masahiro agreed. Nick went down the escalator and out into the day, which had miraculously turned sunny. He turned left, walked to the end of the short block, and crossed the street to take up a waiting position in an alcove near the corner. A woman selling hand-painted neckties off a colorful cart eyed him suspiciously. Nick leaned against the wall and lit a cigarette, keeping his eye on the entrance to the department store.

Almost an hour passed before she came out, carrying a shopping bag emblazoned with the chic colors of the store. She turned to walk in Nick's direction. He watched for Masahiro, who was right behind her. He signaled, holding up his hand with the palm open toward Nick, pushing forward: stay back. Nick stayed back, watching in complete confusion as Masahiro dropped back, too, and Miyuki crossed the street and continued on down the block in the middle of a huge crowd of shoppers and strollers. Masahiro came striding across the street and headed for Nick with an irate expression on his face.

"What the hell's going on?" Nick asked him. "You let her get away?"

"No! I signaled to you to come here, to follow. Didn't you see my hand? I did this . . ." He repeated the gesture. Palm facing Nick, fingers up, pushing toward him.

"In American that means 'stay put,' hot dog!" Nick exclaimed.

Masahiro drew himself up to his full height. "In

Japan it means 'come here,' " he said. "Need I remind you which country you're in? So you see, I was correct."

They stared at each other, frustrated and pooped. "You hot dog," Masahiro said in disgust.

Nick turned away from him. "I cannot work like this, man," he said.

Suddenly Masahiro called out sharply, "Hey, asses and elbows, Conklin!"

Nick turned back. There she was—coming out of a boutique about halfway down the block, standing out from the crowd for just one moment in her elegant black ensemble. Nick and Masahiro made eye contact with each other and Nick took off.

He stayed twenty yards behind her. She was looking in shop windows, taking her time. Masahiro hurried on past Nick, and past Miyuki herself—a man with a place to go. He crossed the avenue and went on about another twenty yards or so, stopping to light a cigarette and study the display in a bookstore window.

Miyuki made the light and crossed the avenue, and then Masahiro picked her up while Nick sauntered on ahead. The two cops were working in perfect sync.

She turned into a bank. Masahiro signaled Nick in the Japanese fashion—and this time Nick understood. It meant "stay back"—exactly the opposite of what it would mean in American—and he stayed back. Masahiro hurried on inside while Nick kept an eye on the front door.

Masahiro lost her inside the bank. She disappeared with an attendant down the stairs where the safe-deposit boxes were kept. He couldn't trail her down there with no reason unless he wanted to blow his cover. He waited and watched the stairs, and many people came and went, but she seemed lost. Just as he was wondering if there could possibly be another exit from the safe-deposit area, he saw her coming up the stairs. But she was wearing a full-length coat now and completely different clothes. High heels, a printed dress and coat—what had happened to the stark black silk pants and jacket? Masahiro was reasonably sure there was no dressing room down in the bank's vault—but there was no time to speculate. He followed her out of the door and signaled to Nick. Startled, Nick picked up on the change and both men took off after her.

Miyuki ran across the middle of the busy commercial avenue, defying traffic and dodging irate horn-pushers. She saw a cab and hailed it, making the driver choose fast between stopping for her or running her down. The cab stopped and a man got out of it. In her haste to get inside, Miyuki brushed against the man, but said nothing and got inside quickly.

Masahiro put his hand up to hail another taxi, but Nick stopped him. "Look—the guy who got out of the cab . . ." he told Masahiro. The man was about to get into another taxi.

"They just pulled a switch," Nick said. Masahiro looked totally baffled. "I recognized him," Nick said. "That's the guy who set Charlie up."

"Let's go," Masahiro said.

The cab ahead of them pulled away with the man in it; they jumped into the next one and went after him.

"What's the switch?" Masahiro pondered. "She must have been downstairs in the safe-deposit vault. What did she take out—she must have handed it to him just then."

"And changed her outfit to throw us off," Nick

concluded. "Tell the driver if he loses that cab I'll kill him with my bare hands."

"I don't think that would help the case, Nick," Masahiro said. "If you don't mind, I think I will not translate."

"Just let's not lose the fucker," Nick muttered.

"Well, that perhaps I will explain to the driver," Masahiro said. He leaned forward and whatever he said worked. The two cabs were practically locking bumpers, but so was everybody else in this traffic.

They wound their way into the heavy industrial area where trucks and cement mixers clogged the streets; the cabs and private cars thinned out a bit, but that hardly meant wide open spaces. There were factories and processing plants and huge storage tanks and acres of parking lots—if it weren't for the omnipresent signs in huge Kenji characters, you might think you were in New Jersey. They moved slowly through the clotted streets, never losing sight of the cab carrying the man who had called himself Nashida.

The taxi turned in at the entrance to a huge busy steel mill. Cars and trucks were streaming in and out, and the gates were wide open; no attention was paid as the two taxis joined the other vehicles and the workers who were hurrying in all directions.

"Stop here," Nick said suddenly. They were in an area between several massive corrugated sheds. Steam pipes and funnels and vast elaborate machinery wormed in and out of the buildings and across the lots between. It would be easier to follow on foot now, easier to see without being seen. Masahiro quickly paid the driver and they sprinted in the direction the other cab had gone.

They saw it at the same time, just pulling up

alongside one of the huge windowless buildings. Nick and Masahiro cut across the yard in a zigzag line, crossing under giant coal conveyors, swerving around steam vents, keeping out of sight. They saw Nashida emerge from the cab and walk left, between two towering blast furnaces. The heat must have hit him like a one-hundred-mile-an-hour gale; from fifty yards away it looked to Nick and Masahiro like the hurrying figure was enveloped in wiggly colorless Jell-O. The heat distorted the air and everything in it. But Nashida kept hurrying along the path until he came to a staircase that climbed the wall of one of the furnace buildings. At the top of the stairs there was a glassed-in area with tables and chairs—a canteen. Nobody could be seen in the room, but Nashida mounted the stairs and went into the room through an unlocked door.

Nick looked higher and spotted a catwalk that ran around the top of the building. If there was a way to get up there, they might have a clear view into the canteen area.

The furnace inside that building was belching fire. The outside walls were too hot to touch and the heat was nearly unbearable as they climbed an emergency staircase on the opposite side of the building. The stairs were steel slats riveted to straight up-and-down poles; if you touched them you'd burn your hands, so the trick was to climb up without holding on to the sides. Masahiro nearly lost his footing but hung on and, with a boost from Nick, who was above him, got back on the vertical track. He didn't mention, then or ever, that his hands were seared and blistering.

They reached the roof and swung onto the narrow catwalk that crisscrossed over the roaring open furnace below. The heat was like a Swedish sauna in the Sahara Desert—the worst either Nick or Masahiro had ever experienced. They moved as quickly as they could along the rail-less catwalk in the direction of the glassed-in room. Finally, sweating so much Nick feared the workers might look up to see if it was raining, they moved beyond the furnace room and over what appeared to be the office section of the building. A huge overhead crane moved up and down, dangerously close. The operator waved at them and proceeded with his work, assuming they had a right to be there. Masahiro gave him his best official nod in return and they went on inching their way along until they were over the canteen itself.

Long metal tables formed rows with straight-backed plastic chairs lined up for the employees' discomfort. All the tables but one were empty just now. At a center table, Sato sat at one end and Sugai at the other. They were glaring at each other. Between them, halfway down the length of the table, sat a mediator. Nashida was there, standing near Sato, and apparently, he had just handed his boss an envelope, which Sato was holding close to his vest. Two of Sugai's lieutenants and Sato's Number One man were guarding the doors and each other.

Nick and Masahiro could see them talking, but it was impossible to hear a word through the glass, with the furnace belching and roaring through the building.

"Banzai," Nick said. "Get to a phone, partner."

Masahiro nodded and headed back down along the hot walk.

21

*A*s Nick watched from high over their heads, Sato and Sugai each placed a hundred-dollar bill down on their respective ends of the bare metal table. One was heads up, the other showed tails. The two men, looking only at each other, turned their bills over. The other sides were blank.

The mediator spoke to each of the men in turn. Sato and Sugai grunted agreement.

Nick got it. Each man had one engravers' plate, and neither was able to mint any more phoneys until one of them got both plates in his possession. Sato must have double-crossed his mentor, but he wouldn't have taken off with only half the goods—he got crossed up in his turn, by the guy whose throat he slit the day he ruined everybody's appetite at Scalari's.

The talk was getting angry down below Nick's

perilous perch. The two warlords were taking turns accusing each other and, apparently, insulting each other. Every now and then one of the armed thugs would take a menacing step forward, only to be waved back to his post by his boss or the mediator. Sato seemed calmer, more in control of the situation than Sugai, but maybe that was just a personality thing. Nick was beginning to realize that beneath the uniformly placid surfaces of the Japanese style, there were as many individual depths as there were in Brooklyn or anywhere else in the world. It was more difficult to spot the differences because they didn't let it all hang out, and what the hell—maybe that wasn't such a bad thing after all. From his observation point, Nick analyzed body language and reactions to get the gist of what they were saying.

Sugai, the elder, the scarred old godfather, was mad as hell at Sato who had grown up, left the nest, and struck out on his own—in competition.

Sato answered his accuser and then, with a slight bow to the mediator, he seemed to be saying something conciliatory. An apology, maybe? Nick doubted it. Sato's arrogance was what made him such a cold-blooded killer. He wouldn't be apologizing for a damn thing, not ever. More likely he was demanding respect and equal status. He had proved he could play hardball, and now he wanted to be co-captain instead of bat-boy.

Whatever he was saying was only making Sugai madder. Maybe he was trying to give him a stroke. The older man, in a sudden fit of rage, stood up, kicking the plastic chair over behind him. He strode the length of the table to where Sato was sitting. Suddenly Sugai whipped his hand back across Sato's face, hard. A deep red bruise started to rise at once, but Sato hadn't even flinched. He just spit out one word, and Nick would have bet the farm he knew what it was.

Sugai walked out of the room, his lieutenants respectfully making way for him and conducting him out. Sato looked at the mediator, as if to say "I told you so." He picked up his heads-only bill and shoved it in his pocket. He left the room with his boys.

Nick crossed a steel beam, balancing and moving forward for four or five feet to get over to an emergency ladder running down the movable crane. He leaped to the moving platform, but he misjudged the distance and ended up hanging on to the edge of the steel beam, dangling a hundred feet over the gigantic vat of bubbling molten steel.

Thank God for the daily workouts in the gym and whoever invented chin-ups. He pulled himself up onto the girder. The crane had swung a bit closer. Nick leaped again and this time he made it to the moving platform. Down below, Sato, Nashida, and Sato's Number One man were three tiny figures moving across the tracks, where a huge crucible stood waiting for a full load of molten waste before it started moving out.

Nick grabbed on to a ladder as the crane began to lower his platform. With explosive white-hot pieces of metal showering all around him, he did some fast-and-fancy broken-field running through an alley of dripping steel girders, keeping his head down and wishing he'd cut down on the hazard by getting a haircut recently. He could smell the singed ends as he ran, or maybe it was burning fibers that meant his clothes had caught fire . . . and then just as suddenly he was out from under. He stopped at a corner where he could shake himself and brush away burning embers and sparks that clung to him.

Cautiously, he peered around the corner—and quickly, he pulled back. Sato and his two cohorts were mounting up on three black motorcycles that were parked facing the open door to the street. The door was still a couple of hundred yards away, but with the bikes—now revving up—they would cover it and be gone from here in a matter of seconds.

Nick stretched around to see if there was any sign of rescue coming, from any direction. He couldn't let Sato drive out of here, lose him again! Where the hell were the Osaka police when you needed them? How the hell long was it taking Masa to find a fucking phone and make a fucking call?

In another second it would be too late. Nick ran forward, staying on the far side of the vat, hoping they wouldn't see him or hear him because getting the drop on the three of them was the only advantage he could hope for. He leaped out into their path.

"Hands where I can see them! NOW!" he shouted.

The reaction was spontaneous and instantaneous— the three cycles launched themselves in separate directions. Nick fired at Sato.

"I won't die because you want me to!" Sato yelled at him over the roar of the bikes in that cavernous caldron. "You have to do it, Conklin!"

Then he shouted something in Japanese to his men. Immediately, their bikes turned a wide arc and headed back behind the furnace on both sides to circle around and surround Nick. He couldn't see them now, but he could still hear Sato loud and clear.

"How much do you want to walk away from here,

Conklin?" Sato taunted him. "Fifty? A hundred thousand? It wouldn't be your first time."

Nick concentrated on trying to get a fix on the voice.

Nashida and the Number One man were yelling at each other in Japanese, getting a fix on him.

"I'm close, Conklin," came Sato's voice again. "Almost as close as when you let Charlie die."

"NICK!"

It was Masahiro. Instinctively, Nick obeyed the sound of it, ducking down low. A shot rang out and a bullet ricocheted off the girder, right where Nick's head had been a split-second before. As he hit the floor, Nick saw some movement ahead of him. Hoping desperately that it wasn't Masahiro, he pulled off a shot. A bike careened crazily as its rider fell off into an unmoving heap. The bike shrieked up against a wall, finally, and sighed and fell over with an echoing crunch of metal and whining dying engine. Sato's Number One man lay absolutely still where he had fallen.

Masahiro hurried to Nick's side. "Sorry, Nick," he said. "Are you all right?"

"Was that your shot that damn near took my head off?"

Masahiro actually blushed. He stared at the dent in the steel girder where his bullet had hit. "I missed him, but you got him, Nick."

"Masa," Nick told him gravely, "you shoot me and I'll kill you."

Bike engines roared up behind them. Nick and Masahiro, still crouching, whirled around. Sato and Nashida were gunning around the obstacle course of pipes and tracks and coal conveyors. Sato fired at

Nick, then Nashida got off a couple, but the steel girders took the brunt of them.

"Get him!" Nick yelled.

Masahiro took off fast, sprinting through the pipes and jumble of equipment. He caught sight of Nashida bolting between two widely placed vats—an easy shot if you were accustomed to this sort of thing. Masahiro took aim and squeezed the trigger. He missed. The wild ricochet took the round from a hit on the broadside of the vat to another dent in another girder, and then like a brilliantly executed billiard shot, it struck Nashida's wrist.

Howling with pain, Sato's boy flew off the bike, flipped over in a somersault through the air, and landed on the hot plates. From where Nick stood— and later Masahiro said the same thing from his angle—it looked like Nashida's body just simply exploded in the thick of the six-hundred-degree steam.

Nick didn't wait around for Nashida's death certificate. He leaped up onto the rim of a coal conveyor and dashed along the top of it, onto another one, and from one to the next, trying to spot Sato and get a shot at him.

Of course, it made him a dead target for Sato, but he had to draw him out. And suddenly, there he was—on his bike and heading for the wide-open doors down at the far end of the shed. Nick sighted and had him, but he didn't shoot.

He couldn't shoot, because in that instant, Sato was surrounded by cyclists. There must have been ten or twelve of them, all in black, all on black bikes, all Sato's protectors, as he geared down and rode easily through the mob.

Sirens could be heard coming closer, arriving outside the building, covering the doors. Nick watched with fierce disappointment as the police cars pulled up, and the cyclists coolly rode past them toward the gates. Once on the street outside the steel mill, Sato took the lead of his pack, twisting the throttle and—gone.

Nick sprinted toward the door, screaming blue murder and leveling his pistol, seriously meaning to kill every fuck-up cop in Japan for letting Sato waltz away right under their noses.

In a blind-side tackle that knocked the wind out of him and cracked his head on the cement floor, Nick found himself looking up into the barrel of a revolver. A tough young uniformed cop, who looked like he'd been practicing looking evil in front of the mirror at home, was holding the gun about two inches from Nick's forehead. Suddenly Nick's arms were jerked behind him and a second young warrior cop was cuffing him. Japanese handcuffs are made for small wrists and they cut into Nick's flesh as they were snapped shut.

"Jesus, man!" he yelped. "I'm on your side . . . for God's sake, listen to me!"

Impassive, the two officers hustled him to his feet and half-shoved, half-dragged him across the mill floor to the open doorway where Superintendent Ohashi was standing. Nick, covered with sweat and dirt, gasped for breath and stumbled, but he was in a bigger hurry than they were and he managed to stay on his feet.

The minute he caught sight of Ohashi, he yelled out, "If your people are spread out, there's still a chance you can stop him!"

Ohashi stood impassive and silent. Nick damned near exploded. "Get these fucking cuffs off me!" he roared.

Finally, Ohashi barked an order to the two cops who were holding Nick. But instead of freeing him, they shoved him outside, toward a police car pulled up tight against the building.

"What the hell are you doing?!" Nick raged.

In perfect English, Ohashi told him. "We're going to put you on a plane back to New York, nonstop. If you return, you will be arrested."

Masahiro had been standing there the whole time, with a pained look on his face.

"For God's sake, Masa!" Nick pleaded from the back of the car.

Masahiro opened his mouth to speak, but Ohashi silenced him with one curt word. Then the superintendent turned and went about his business as if Masahiro didn't even exist—not to mention Nick Conklin.

They drove him straight to the airport, where it had all begun. The day turned dark, and somewhere along the highway, it became night. When they pulled into the departure area, the cops made sure of the plane and the gate and security on their radio before they ever left the car. While they hustled Nick, still painfully cuffed, out of the car and through the terminal to the gate, he searched frantically over the crowds and commotion for some way out. Where were the fake cops when you needed them?

They took him through the gate, up the gangway, into the plane. The cops had an animated conversation with the flight attendants. Nick looked around the plane—it was a 747 and packed to the gills. A few emotionless faces stared back at him. One of the cops handed some papers to a flight attendant, then his escort led Nick to a seat in the midsection of the plane across from the galley. Probably so the flight attendants could keep an eye on him in case he decided to hijack the plane or bail out at a hundred thousand feet.

Everyone in the immediate vicinity scrutinized him with obvious distaste. He was not only the only *gaigin* on the plane, he was filthy, covered with dirt and grime from the steel mill. Some stared openly, others stole sideways glances and quickly looked away when Nick looked back at them. It didn't help that the uniformed cop was standing over him like he had orders to shoot to kill and was just dying to try them out.

A flight attendant came up to tell his keeper it was time to leave. The cop uncuffed Nick and handed him his passport, said something in Japanese that was doubtlessly unflattering, and left the plane. Nick watched the attendants shut and seal the doors. The sound cut through him with a finality that sank like a block of cement right down through his chest and gut to his socks. There was no way out now. Charlie was gone and he was on his way home with a shitload of failure and disgrace, not to mention the fucking Internal inquisition.

The squawkbox came on with the usual fascinating information about the plane and the flight and how to save your life if it took a dive—all in Japanese. A stewardess with a thick wad of bills in one hand came down the aisle collecting cash for the headphones.

Nick looked out the window. Baggage was being loaded right under him. Suitcases, duffels, cartons—

and Charlie Vincent's coffin. He watched as four handlers struggled to hoist it inside the belly of the plane. The baggage truck, empty, pulled away. The luggage hatch was slammed and sealed with another kind of finality.

The magazines in the rack ahead of him were all in Japanese. Outside the window, it was dark and the service vehicles were still fussing around the plane. Nick looked over at the galley area.

There was a steward in there busily unloading trays of food from a little elevator. Opposite the galley there was an exit door, but Nick knew if he tried unlatching it the escape slides would be activated and the alarms would go off. The stew finished unloading the trays and punched a button to send the elevator down. He stowed the food cart with its full load into the cooler and headed down the aisle.

Nick glanced out the window again. The catering truck was loading the last of the food into the plane's innards. He looked down the aisle, where all the flight attendants were busily stowing overhead baggage, handing out headsets, plumping pillows, calming nervous passengers, answering questions.

Quick as the wind, Nick rose from his seat and ducked into the galley area. He pushed the elevator button. It only took a few seconds for the small elevator to arrive, and no one saw him squeeze into it, punch the Down button from the outside, and pull the door shut.

The door opened automatically when it reached the loading level. Two of the catering crew were on the ground, moving the trays and cartons from the van to the plane; one man was crouched with his back to Nick at the edge of the loading hatch, and as Nick hunched over in the dark belly of the plane, watching them, the last man jumped down from the hatch and all three climbed into their van.

Nick ran to the hatch, lowered himself out and down onto the tarmac. He hunkered down behind the huge wheel of the 747, praying he hadn't been spotted. The catering truck pulled away.

The jet engines blasted as the pilot turned on each in turn to test them. Nick figured he'd be permanently deaf for the rest of his life.

Squatting low and staying in the shadows, he ran for cover toward the darkening wing of a terminal building that looked closed-up for the night. Behind him, the 747 rolled out slowly and headed for the runway.

22

Staying close to the wall of the building and keeping an eye out for a night watchman, he moved in the direction of the airport access road, away from the lights and crowds of the main passenger terminals. He had to walk a couple of miles in pitch darkness alongside the road—the trick was to use the headlights from the traffic but not to let them pick him out—before he finally found a roadside telephone booth.

He made his call and waited in the booth, out of the mist which was turning into a heavy dull rain. There were some vending machines next to the phone booth, but everything looked like dried fish to him so he ignored his gnawing appetite and kept hoping no cars would pull into the lay-by while he was still hanging around. Mist shrouded the narrow, two-lane road that ran along the far perimeter of the airport. A high chain-link fence lined both sides of the road.

The rain was pelting down hard now and Nick could barely make out the lights of a slow-moving car as it came toward the airport. A huge truck flashed its lights and sounded its air horn as it passed the car with a whoosh of rainwater. The car glided to a halt under the single road-light that marked the turnoff where Nick waited. The car idled for a moment. Nick, his fingers crossed, jogged over to it.

The passenger door swung open. The most beautiful blonde he had ever hoped to see was at the wheel. Dripping wet, he got inside and had to restrain himself from kissing her.

"I wasn't sure you were coming," he told Joyce.

She didn't answer, but ground the car into gear and pulled out onto the road, making a turn to head back to town.

"Thanks," Nick said.

She was accelerating as fast as the little sedan would go. She shifted hard. She didn't seem to feel the need to say anything at all. Nick was surprised and a little dismayed. Was she pissed off? But she had come for him. He blotted his dripping face with his soaked sleeve.

"I have to find Matsumoto, then get to Sugai—" he said.

Joyce interrupted him. "Don't push it. You're lucky I picked up the phone."

She was right. She owed him nothing; less than nothing—in fact it was the other way around. And she was sticking her neck out.

"I'm sorry," he said softly, meaning it. "I do

appreciate it. You can just drop me off in town somewhere."

Joyce shot him a sideways glance. Not really unfriendly. "They'll pick you up in a minute," she said.

She leaned forward to wipe the windshield with a grimy rag. Then she tossed it in his lap.

"You can do whatever you want to when I'm clear of you," she told him. "For now, you'll go where I take you."

Nick couldn't figure her yet, not at all. "Where's that?" he asked cautiously.

"Somewhere you'll be safe," she said.

Nick put his head back against the seat, which was so short that his head went all the way back and he was staring at the roof of her car—and that was only inches away from his nose. He shut his eyes and sighed. There was no point in arguing with her, he could see that. Maybe a little safety would be all right until he figured out exactly what the hell to do.

He watched her profile while she drove until she told him he was making her nuts, and then he watched the lights of Osaka getting closer and brighter until they were all around them.

It was called The Love Hotel and it was a lot more elegant than its name. A ramp over a lighted pool led to a lobby where subdued lighting and soft music vied with the rhythmic babbling of a little waterfall to soothe your tired nerves. A young couple were negotiating with a well-dressed clerk at the registration desk.

"What's it going to be?" Joyce asked Nick. "Every room's a specialty. How about a girls' school? No? Paris by night? Swinging from the vines?"

"They got Tarzan?" Nick queried dubiously. Was she putting him on or what?

He had a little trouble believing his eyes when they got to the room. It was a jungle theme, all right, with pretty real-looking plastic trees, vines hanging down and crossing the ceiling, stuffed animals peeking out from leaves and hanging from branches. It was comical and absurd and Nick could only guess at some of the antics that must have gone on there.

"They sure go to ends to make the hookers happy," he said. "All you get in New York is a towel."

Joyce shook her head and smiled. "Married couples come here," she told him. "They want a little fantasy and a little privacy. This country has thin walls . . ."

Nick shrugged. "Strange people," he said.

Joyce unloaded her shoulder bag onto the double bed. "And you make a world of goddamned sense, I suppose?" she asked him, rougher than she meant it to sound. Against her better judgment, she liked him. More than liked him, he sensed. She dug into her bag and came up with a covered *bento* box and a handful of yen. "Here's some food," she said, handing him the boxed lunch, "and some cash. You've got the room till morning."

"I know you're taking a risk doing this," Nick told her. "I appreciate it . . ." Words seemed stupid and inadequate.

Joyce zipped up her coat. She was going to leave.

"What about Sugai?" Nick asked her. "Can I find him at the club?"

"No," Joyce said.

She looked at him for a long time, and then—also apparently, against her better judgment—she took a piece of paper and pen from her bag and wrote down an address. She handed him the paper. "You want

Sugai," she said, "this is where you'll find him. He's a big golfer. Goes here three nights a week."

She went to the phone book and looked up Matsumoto Masahiro's home address. She copied it out for him in English and Japanese. Then she grabbed up her bag and slung it over her shoulder.

Nick touched her arm. "You know," he said, "you always want to be rid of me, but then there you are. We ought to figure that out sometime."

"There's nothing to figure," she said. "You're a thick-headed, cocky American trying to do the right thing, and you're also determined to get yourself killed." She took a couple of steps toward the door.

Nick grinned and reached up for one of the vines. "The room is paid for till morning," he reminded her.

She turned back, but only for a minute. Nodding at the vines and a little stuffed crocodile on the bed, she said, "It's the right place, but it's the wrong time. I'll let you know when—if ever."

She stepped into his arms and kissed his mouth, a caring, passionate kiss, hard and long. He was stunned but reacted in the only way he could.

"You said you weren't going to be any more trouble, remember?" she said, touching his face affectionately. He understood, suddenly, what this was about. She didn't think he was going to be alive much longer.

"Goodbye, Nick," she said.

She walked out of the door, closing it gently behind her.

"Fabulous." Nick sighed out loud.

He was so hungry he ate everything in the *bento* box except the raw ginger. He was amazed at his prowess with the chopsticks, although there were a couple of moments, featuring his fingers, to indicate that he might not be quite ready for a public performance. He showered in the tiny cubicle for about a half-hour, until he started feeling clean again, and then he fell into the jungle bed and slept so deeply he didn't hear a thing when Joyce came back to leave dry clothes hanging from one of the trees for him.

It was several hours later when he swam up from the deep sleep and realized he felt like himself again. When he walked out of The Love Hotel, alone, feeling only a little foolish, he hailed a cab and showed the driver the paper on which Joyce had written Masahiro's address.

The district was distinguished only by the rows and rows of tall and uniformly neat but dingy apartment buildings. Tiny balconies swarmed with laundry, bird cages, plants and flowers both real and artificial. Entering Masahiro's building, he had to step over bicycles that cluttered the halls. The building resounded with the lively sounds of family life going on behind every door. Nick checked the piece of paper and found the apartment with the number Joyce had written down. He knocked.

The door opened a crack. A pair of steely eyes peered out at Nick. A muscular young man in suit and tie stood glaring at the *gaigin* at his door.

"Konichi-wa," Nick stuttered. *Hi.* "Matsumoto Masahiro?" Or was it the other way around?

The young man did not respond but he stepped aside to let Nick enter. The main room of the apartment was tiny and drab to the point of making his own dump seem like a palace in comparison. A television was blaring a jangling, indecipherable game show. The young man paid no attention to either Nick or the TV. He went to a corner which served as a cooking area and began clattering around with pots and pans.

Nick waited. Nothing. There was another room, from which he could hear strains of stereo music between the hee-haws of the game show. He went to the door and looked inside. It was a very small bedroom, with a bedroll laid out on the floor and a low desk against the opposite wall. Masahiro sat at the desk, cross-legged on the floor, with his back to Nick. He was practicing calligraphy with delicate strokes on a scroll of rice paper. There were a bottle of ink and a jar holding an assortment of brushes on the desk, as well as a half-full bottle of Suntory. The stereo was playing a string quartet.

"Masa . . ." Nick said quietly.

Masahiro turned and saw Nick. Clearly, he assumed he was seeing an apparition. "It is not possible. You are gone," he said.

All of a sudden, Masahiro seemed small, frail, and broken to Nick. He spoke gently to the older man. "You know me," he said with a rueful little smile, "I never come along quietly. I came back for you. I need your help."

Masahiro reached up to turn off the stereo. The sound of the game show bled in obscenely from the next room. He went back to his work.

"It would be better if you had not come," he said. "I am sorry."

The young man entered the bedroom, carrying a tray with a teapot and a bowl of steaming soup. He looked at Nick.

"You have done enough to him," he said in heavily accented high-school English. Then he turned to his father and his voice softened as he offered him tea in their own language.

Masahiro spoke sharply to his son, who did not answer. He put down the tray and left the room.

"Please pardon my son," Masahiro said. "He came to comfort me. But all he does is show his disappointment."

Nick heard the front door slam. He saw Masahiro flinch involuntarily, almost as if he had been shot.

"You never told me you had a son," Nick said.

"Does not matter." Masahiro shook his head as if to clear it. He looked at Nick with tired eyes. "I have been suspended, Nick. I am no longer Assistant Inspector."

Nick sat down on a *tatami* mat on the floor. He leaned his head back against the wall and thought about what this meant to the other man. "Christ, Masa, I'm sorry," he said.

"I knew what I was doing," Masahiro said. "I deserve the disgrace."

Nick shook his head. "It's not over," he said. "I want to use Sugai to get us close to Sato. We can still get him—you and me."

"I cannot help you, Nick," Masahiro said sadly. "Look at me."

Nick stood up, ready to get going. "We can fix everything," he insisted.

"I am not like you. For a moment I thought I could be." Masahiro was dangerously close to destroyed, and needed careful handling—which did not mean coddling.

Nick noticed a Buddhist altar in the corner of the room. On it were an old photo of a woman in a kimono, some burnt-down joss sticks, and Charlie's Zippo lighter.

"You didn't do anything wrong," Nick said. "You kicked ass."

"It is for nothing," Masahiro said.

"Masa—"

"I didn't lose only a job, Nick. I lost everything. I belonged to a group. They will not have me anymore."

Nick sighed. "So what are you going to do?" he asked.

"I am nothing," Masahiro told him.

"It's up to you," Nick said. "Listen, I'm in worse shape than you. Your cops are looking for me; I've been deported and I'm still here, and when I get home they're going to skin me alive and hang me out to dry. You don't see me rolling over, though, do you?"

Masahiro tried to smile, didn't make it. "Just go," he said.

"You're digging yourself a real hole here, Masa," Nick told him.

"Get out." Masahiro would not look at him. Nick stood for a moment, but there was nothing more he could say. He turned and walked out, past the idiot game show that was blathering hysterically to itself in an empty room.

23

*T*he address Joyce had given him for Sugai turned out to be a driving range on the outskirts of the city. Nick's cabbie grumbled and mumbled to himself all the way, and then charged a lot more than was on the meter—either there was a surcharge for going off the main drag or the guy was a *gonif* (not Japanese but Brooklynese for "thief"). Nick paid with the money Joyce had thoughtfully provided. If he got out of this the way he hoped, the NYPD would pick up the tab; if he didn't—well, no point in dwelling on life's gloomier possibilities.

The driving range was just off the highway and lit with the inevitable neon—an animated sign that showed a swinging golf club endlessly hitting a bright white ball that sailed across the sign, only to reappear as the whole process started again.

Nick took his time casing the place. There were

three levels where customers could pay for a bucket of balls and hit them from a brightly lit row of tees out into the darkness hundreds of yards away. The lower two levels were filled with scores of people, mostly men, lined up and whacking away. Nick climbed the stairs to the top level. It was deserted except for one player—Sugai. Three of his boys were with him, not driving golf balls, just watching. One must have weighed four hundred pounds and it didn't look like much of it was fat, either. He had his eye on Nick.

Nick reached the top of the steps and headed across the walkway that crossed behind the driving tees. It was a high platform, raised the equivalent of several stories above the busy highway below. The monstrous man—who must have been a *sumo* wrestler—moved toward Nick on amazingly agile feet. Nick allowed himself to be overtaken. They stopped a good thirty yards from where Sugai was now leaning on his driver and looking pained at the intrusion.

"Sugai, I've got something for you!" Nick called out. He started to reach into his pocket but the *sumo* champ tightened his hold on Nick's arm. "Ease up, pal," Nick told him. "Here, you give him this."

He reached with his free hand into his inside jacket pocket. The *sumo* twisted Nick's arm behind his back and pushed him toward the edge of the walkway until the tips of Nick's shoes were over the edge. Then he reached into Nick's pocket with a hand the size of a waffle iron and came up with the envelope. He handed it to the second thug, who had moved in close. Number Two carried it over to Sugai and handed it to him.

Sugai, who had gone back to driving golf balls, stopped and opened the envelope. He pulled out the hundred-dollar bill, and without hesitation or change of expression, handed it back to his lieutenant. He resumed his game.

Nick was still standing precariously over the edge of the walkway, his balance held only by the whim of the mean green giant. Sugai looked up casually from his golf ball—sort of an afterthought—and gave a single brief nod. Holy shit, Nick thought, he's telling him to drop me over. The steady flow of traffic flashing by on the highway below made the whole platform rumble.

But the *sumo* wrestler pulled Nick back with one rough jerk of his hand. He pushed and shoved and kicked Nick over to the stairs and down. Near the bottom of the staircase Nick lost his footing, and the *sumo* picked him up with one hand as if he were a bag of straw.

Nick was half-kicked and half-carried to the parking lot and thrown head-first into the back seat of a car. The *sumo* didn't close the door but he didn't get in either. He just stood there with his hands on his enormous hips and stared at Nick. There was no one else in the car.

"Am I driving?" Nick asked.

The monstrous hand swatted him on the side of the head—again and again and again—powerful blows that made his whole body ring with pain.

Two of Sugai's boys appeared from nowhere and climbed into the front seat. The *sumo* got in alongside Nick and slammed the door as hard as he had just been slamming Nick. Another tough-and-ugly got in on the other side of Nick, and the guy behind the wheel started out of the parking lot. They headed back toward the city.

With his head throbbing and blood trickling out of

his ear, Nick still managed to concentrate on where they were heading. They drove in a wide circle, then doubled back and circled again. Killing time? Trying to confuse him? He didn't see the point, but he wasn't too surprised when they finally pulled into the walled estate outside which he and Masahiro had spent the long night waiting for the girl. The tour of the city must have been to give his host a chance to get there before they brought him in. Stay cool, Nick. Ignore the screaming pain inside your head. Watch for tricks.

The approach to Sugai's mansion was an immaculately tended gravel driveway edged with low lights carefully placed to highlight the expanse of lawn and formal stone gardens. The car stopped and the thugs pushed Nick out. The doors opened from within, double doors in polished teak with glowing brass hinges and bell.

With a start, Nick recalled Charlie reading to him from the guidebook about something called a Nightingale Corridor that the ancient wealthy Japanese had in their castles, a very early-warning sort of burglar alarm approach that signaled to those inside whenever anyone walked through it. The entry to Sugai's house was a Nightingale Corridor—each step on the immaculate wooden floor produced a sound like birdsong.

It sounded more like a whole herd of squawking ducks as the four heavies led Nick down the long corridor to a set of double *shoji* screens at the other end. The thugs slid out of their shoes and signaled Nick to do the same. Then one of the guards slid the screens open and they stepped inside a room which made Nick gasp with inadvertent admiration.

The austere beauty of Imperial Japan lived in this room of burnished woods, deep black lacquerware, and soft, diffused light. Water could be heard running in the garden; the sound served to make the silence resonate.

Sugai, wearing a starched kimono, was seated behind a low table of gleaming black ebony. A male secretary stood behind him holding papers. Sugai looked up but did not acknowledge Nick's presence in any way. He just looked at him like he might watch a tank of tropical fish. Big Boy forced Nick down into a sitting position on the *tatami* mat. Sugai went back to affixing his fine *hanko* to some papers.

"You should be somewhere over the Pacific now, Conklin," he said finally. "We should be rid of you."

"I missed my plane," Nick told him.

Sugai did not appreciate or even understand sarcasm. In his lifestyle not too many people messed with him, as a rule.

"Do you have any idea who I am?" he asked Nick coldly. The burn scars twisted his face into a permanent leer.

"Sure," Nick said.

"No," Sugai told him. He gestured for his secretary to leave, and the man bowed himself out of the room. Then Sugai took the hundred-dollar bill from somewhere inside the folds of his kimono and laid it on the table. "If you did, you wouldn't have given me this," he said.

"It's good stuff," Nick said. "Your friends in New York must be getting anxious."

Sugai was not impressed. He slid the bill into the brazier that warmed his tea. It burned.

"This is an old bill," he said. "A prototype. The new ones will be like everything we make—perfect."

"Who's going to make the profit, you or Sato?" Nick challenged him. "He's got one of your plates. You've got nothing."

Sugai sighed and nodded. "He might as well be an American," he commented coldly. "His kind respects only one thing—money."

"And what are you doing it for—love?" Nick retorted.

He reached into his jacket pocket and pulled out a pack of cigarettes, tapped one out, and lit it. Sugai glanced at the *sumo* champ. Instantly, the cigarette was knocked out of Nick's mouth onto the floor. Nick reached for it and the *sumo* stomped his hand. It hurt like hell but Nick didn't let it show. One of the other thugs quickly picked up the butt before it could singe the floor. He left the room with it and returned a second later without it.

Sugai glared at Nick. He spoke slowly and deliberately. "I was ten when the bombers came. My family lived underground for three days. When we came up, the city was gone. Soon the heat brought the rain . . . black rain . . . you made the rain black. Then you shoved your values down our throats. We who managed to survive forgot who we were. You created Sato and thousands like him. I am paying you back."

Nick nodded, but he was all business. "You want your plate? Get me close to him."

Sugai shook his head. "You have no part in this. I promised the other bosses there would be peace."

"Screw them," Nick said.

"I'm bound by duty and honor," Sugai told him, not expecting him to understand. "If you had time I would explain what that means," he added. As far as he was concerned, the talk was over.

Nick persisted. "I'm the solution to all your problems," he said. "I'll take Sato. Who better than a worthless *gaigin?* Everyone knows he killed my partner. I'll do it and you come out with your honor intact."

"Yes," Sugai said. "He killed your partner, right in front of you. So? I am not impressed."

"Get me close," Nick pleaded. "I'll leave my mark and you'll be clean."

Sugai stared at him for a while before answering. "Why should I trust you?" he asked.

Nick shrugged. "Because you've got nothing to lose," he said.

"I shall think on this," Sugai said. "You will wait." With a slight motion of his hand he dismissed Nick. His guards pulled him to his feet and barreled him out of the room.

The rooms of the enormous house were set at square angles so that many private interior courtyards and gardens were formed. Nick was escorted out into one of the gardens. Wooden benches were placed under the overhanging eaves of the house, and it was a good thing because it had started to rain again. Nick huddled on a bench watching the patterns of water dripping onto the set stones and the grassy areas, running down a trough to feed the flower beds. Two of Sugai's men flanked him on their own benches, keeping their eyes on him. Even though he had no wish to go, he was clearly Sugai's prisoner.

The brisk night air and the fresh feeling of the rain helped, at first, to clear the worst of the stabbing pain from Nick's head. But after a couple of hours it was just cold and damp and miserable. The charm of the formal Japanese garden was starting to elude him after all.

And then one of the *shoji* doors slid open across the courtyard and Sugai, without the kimono and wearing wooden clogs with his business suit, came toward Nick. A man with a crew cut scurried alongside, holding an umbrella high over his boss.

"First you will sleep, then you will be taken to him," Sugai told Nick.

Nick nodded and followed the parade into a different wing of the house. He was given tea and cake, a hot bath, and a bedroll in a room to himself—if you didn't count the guard inside the room and the two guards outside the room at the inside door and the door to the garden. He didn't actually sleep much.

At five A.M. they came for him. He was squeezed into the back of the car again, with a different man on either side of him and two in front. They were all sprucely dressed in the *Yakuza* "uniform"—crisp pressed dark suits, white shirts, dark ties, and large sunglasses. Nick found himself looking into the barrel of a sawed-off shotgun. The man in the front passenger seat was pointing it at him. Nick was so mesmerized by the unexpected sight that he failed to note a car parked just outside the gates of Sugai's house.

24

Sugai was behind them all the way in a smooth black chauffeured Cadillac. The two cars drove into the countryside for miles, off the highway onto smaller roads and finally dirt roads which had turned to mud in the rain. Just as dawn was clearing the horizon they came to a terraced hillside and stopped.

The door of the Caddy opened and a bodyguard got out, made way for Sugai who followed. Another guard from Sugai's seemingly endless supply got out and flanked him carefully. The rain had stopped, but the guard held a furled umbrella, just in case.

The man in the front seat who had held the shotgun trained on Nick the entire way got out and motioned for Nick to get out too.

Sugai pointed to a farmhouse in the middle distance, just visible in the first light of day. Dim lights glowed through the windows of the house. "Four *Oyabuns* will arrive here shortly with their body-guards," he told Nick. "Sato will also have a lieutenant."

Nick stared at the house and cased the situation as best he could. "A weapon," he said.

Sugai said nothing. The shotgun was still pointing at Nick's head.

"A way in," Nick said. "A way out."

There was still no answer.

"A car," Nick said, hoping the growing desperation didn't leak out of his voice.

Sugai said something in Japanese to one of his men, who whipped out a revolver and tossed it down at Nick's feet. Sugai and his men climbed back into the Cadillac. Nick picked up the gun. It was unloaded and useless.

The first car moved out, and the Cadillac started up right behind it. Nick stood alone on the hillside, holding the empty gun. As the Cadillac accelerated past him, two empty magazines and a handful of cartridges were tossed out the door. They scattered all over the hillside, and by the time Nick had picked it all up, the tail lights of the cars had disappeared down the road.

Nick stayed close to the ground as the daylight came up. He watched the farmhouse across the small valley. A few lights showed through windows and *shoji* screens. A few workers—six, he counted—were working in the terraced fields of the area, and small fires dotted the hillsides.

Two rumpled, lightly armed (as far as he could tell) retainers patrolled the front of the farmhouse compound. An old woman came out of the house to bring them their morning tea.

Nick took off his leather jacket and began to tear strips of cloth from the lining. He tied them around the muzzle and action of his weapon to protect it from mud. He used several strips to make a sling for the revolver in lieu of a holster.

A man with a rifle came along the road down below and stopped. He stayed there, standing guard. In a moment, three other guards took up positions, spreading out down the length of the road leading into the compound. Suddenly the sound of a car broke the morning stillness, and Nick watched a sedan tearing down the road that cut through the little valley.

He didn't hesitate. He started down the hillside, on his belly, rolling from mudhole to rut, staying low to avoid being spotted by the guards or the scattered farm workers.

Much closer to the compound, Nick squatted in a clump of low grass and watched as the sedan pulled up to the gate. Guards stamped out their cigarette butts and straightened their clothes, bowed to the passengers and opened the gates.

Suddenly Nick heard a rustling sound in the grass behind him. Whirling around, he saw a farm worker standing a few yards up the slope, gawking down at him in amazement. The peasant opened his mouth to call out to the guards, but then he decided to groan softly and sink to the ground instead. His hoe went flying.

Nick had instinctively grabbed his gun and now it was trained on the man who had dealt the worker the karate chop to the back of his neck.

"If you pull it, you should use it," Masahiro said.

Nick couldn't believe his eyes. He was even more surprised at how glad he was to see Masahiro. He quickly pulled him down before their position was revealed to the whole countryside. Masahiro landed in the mud, which didn't please him. He started brushing uselessly at his neat suit and the flecks of mud that had splattered on Charlie's tie.

"Sorry, pal," Nick said. "Uh, didn't I hear you say your debt was paid?"

Masahiro wiped at Charlie's tie. "It is," he assured Nick, "but I was suspended from one group. So I decided to join another."

Nick appreciated what it must have taken to get Masahiro there. "Thanks," he said simply.

Masahiro nodded. He looked down at the compound, the guards along the road. "You're going to kill Sato," he said.

"I'll take him any way he makes me," Nick answered.

Masahiro looked at Nick. "Sugai will never let you live," he said.

Nick knew that. "You can walk away, Masa," he said softly.

Masahiro thought about that and then he said, "Whatever happens, that will be all right with me."

Nick shook his head. "I can't rely on someone who wants to die," he said.

"You can rely on someone who's willing to die," Masahiro corrected him.

It was a point that was hard to argue with.

They inched closer to the compound until they reached a wooded spot on the lower terraces of the hillside where they could get a reasonably clear view of the road and the walls of the house. Nick and Masahiro had penetrated road security, but were stuck for the moment.

They watched and waited. Sounds of cars approaching. And then a motorcade of five large American cars wound their way along the narrow road against the sun which was now a fireball rising low in the sky. The cars, all with opaque windows, swept past them and up to the gate.

Men, among them Sugai and his gorillas, piled out of the cars and watched while some of the guards checked thoroughly inside the trunks and under the hoods, beneath the chassis using mirrors mounted on poles. The bodyguards surrendered their weapons to a guard who dropped them in a basket. The drivers and *Oyabuns* were gone over with an electronic "frisk 'em" device. Nick kind of enjoyed watching Sugai submit to that.

The man who had arrived earlier ("the mediator," Masahiro explained to Nick) greeted each of the bosses in turn, then he headed inside the farmhouse and they followed him respectfully. The lieutenants all stayed outside the house, deploying themselves every fifty yards along the road. In the farmyard, the old woman came out with a huge basket of freshly washed linens and began to hang them to dry in the morning sun.

"Sato's not here yet," Nick told Masahiro.

"No. He is the one with the power just now, he will make his entrance importantly," Masahiro said.

And there it was—the distinctive *va-rooooommmmm* of motorcycles approaching. In a second they saw Sato's limo tearing up the dried-mud road with two outriders on street bikes as escort. They passed very close to where Nick and Masahiro were hiding, and they could clearly see the flash of long-blade knives hanging in scabbards from the bikes' forks.

"Fabulous," Nick murmured to himself.

By now Masahiro understood that Nick meant exactly the opposite.

Sato pulled up to the gate with a screech of brakes. He climbed out of his car and his driver came around to walk beside him. They approached the group of drivers and guards for a moment of heated discussion. Evidently, Sato's driver didn't want to hand over his weapon, but he did, finally. Sato allowed himself to be electronically frisked. The device emitted a howl as it passed over his body.

Sato held out a small rectangular package. The plate. The guard took it, finished the frisk, and handed the package back to him. Sato went inside.

Nick started moving closer, with Masahiro right behind him. A guard walked past only a few dozen yards away. They waited and then crept on again until they were at the very edge of the wooded area bordering the farmyard.

"Let's go," he whispered.

"Inside?" Masahiro whispered back, astounded. "Why?"

Nick gestured toward the basket of confiscated guns nestled under the watchful nose of a guard. "Because the sign says check your guns at the door," he said.

Masahiro looked at the compound doubtfully. It was crawling with armed guards.

"It's as close to a sure thing as we're going to get," Nick told him.

Masahiro thought about it for a second. "Let's go," he whispered.

They stayed on the edge of the wooded side of the field as they made their way toward the back of the compound. Farmers worked the land here, trying to wrest every possible foot of arable soil from the hillside. As they moved cautiously through the woods, they were abruptly brought to a halt, frozen in their tracks, by the sight of a farmer sitting on a rock. His cloak and hat were on the ground and he appeared to be resting. But he was dead, a tiny bullet hole in the back of his skull.

They continued inching their way around the compound. Behind the farmhouse, the rough terrain itself had made the building appear to be inaccessible. A stone wall rose ten feet to the deck at the rear of the house. Wooden uprights and beams supported the deck. A single guard patrolled it and the broad expanse of field beyond as well. He was heavily armed with a rifle slung over his shoulder, daggers in his boots, and at least one holster with a gun that was visible. As they watched him, the guard appeared to hear something—he stopped in his tracks and surveyed the landscape. After a moment, he decided it was nothing and Nick and Masahiro started to breathe again.

They stayed frozen against the high stone wall until the guard walked on, and then Nick quickly led the way under the deck. They crouched and listened to the guard's footsteps over their heads. Nick grabbed one of the posts and pulled himself up until he was able to find a toehold on the stone wall. He reached down and grabbed Masahiro's hand, pulled him up.

Nick peered over the wall to the level of the deck. The guard had his back to them, scanning the fields. Silently and swiftly, Nick climbed over and came up behind the guard until he was close enough to ring the guard's head with his arm, pulling his weapon across the man's throat. He tightened his hold and held the man's thrashing feet off the deck until he stopped struggling. Nick let the strangled man down onto the deck without a sound. He and Masahiro quickly moved inside the back door of the farmhouse.

They could hear the voices in the next room through the paper walls. Masahiro translated for Nick, moving his mouth without making a sound.

"The mediator is saying 'you will control trucking and the wholesale market. You will have the Hawaiian dock workers.' Sato agrees, then he asks for the plate. Sugai says, 'Only after you show us your sincerity and loyalty.' Nick, I know what they do now, it is bloody but interesting to watch."

"I don't think we better try to get seats in there for the show," Nick whispered. "Just tell me about it."

"The mediator will remove a cloth cover from a lacquer tray on which will be already placed a small scalpel, some white gauze, and a bottle of clear alcohol. Sato will wrap his finger in the cloth, pick up the knife and spread his fingers and slice off the tip of his right finger—this one—but never taking his eyes off Sugai. He will hand the fingertip wrapped in the white gauze cloth to his boss to signify his loyalty, and if Sugai accepts, he will put the finger in the alcohol to keep as a forever pledge."

"Cute," Nick murmured.

"Shhhh," Masahiro said. "Now the mediator calls for the plate to be handed over."

"Sato couldn't be loyal if his life depended on it," Nick commented.

"It does," Masahiro pointed out.

They looked at each other with the same thought. Sato had some move up his sleeve.

"Shhhh," Masahiro said. "The mediator now is saying that the plates are side-by-side together for the first time. He says to Sato, 'You'll have respect and territory.' He says to Sugai, 'You'll have security and brotherhood.' Now they will drink *sake* to toast the bargain . . . wait . . . Sugai asks Sato why he is not drinking!"

There was a dramatic pause and then a sudden sliding open of a door in the next room, and Sato's loud voice raised in a shout. "He says, 'I'll drink to your funeral,'" Masahiro told Nick, wide-eyed.

Suddenly there was a hideous scream from Sugai, an old man's pathetic howl of pain. All the other *Oyabuns* were exclaiming in rage and horror, and above the commotion—Sato's triumphant cry.

Masahiro didn't take the time to translate. He gestured to Nick, a finger across his throat. The next sound Nick heard from the other room was a bolt being thrown on a gun that meant business. That was all he had to hear. He went crashing right through the paper wall, and in the millisecond of surprise advantage, he zeroed in on a farm worker standing in the doorway aiming a carbine at Sugai. Nick fired and hit him and the man dropped to the floor. He was wearing all the clothes of a farm worker except for his shoes, which were definitely the pointy-toed city-slicker type favored by Sato's goons.

He wasn't quite dead. He roused himself to fire off the rest of his ammo, sporadically and erratically around the room. The bosses scattered and ran for the protection of their guards, who met them on the way in, with great confusion.

Only Sugai and Sato didn't move. Sugai's hand had been impaled to the table with a dagger through it. Sato just stood there staring in disbelief at Nick and Masahiro. He was unarmed. One of his fingers was wrapped in gauze. With his good hand, he reached for the counterfeiting plates. Sugai, mustering the last of his old man's strength, pulled the knife from his own skewered hand and sliced into Sato. Sato dived through the *shoji* wall of the house.

He hit the ground hard and rolled to his feet. From the road and the hillside, his men came running at the sight of him. One of them opened fire on the other guards inside the compound, who were trying to protect their frightened employers running every which way but out. Sato's bikers mounted their cycles and started circling around him, opening holes for him to move any way he wanted to.

Nick and Masahiro rolled out of the building into the raging gunfire. They ran for cover under the eaves of the nearest outbuilding.

"Are you all right?" Masahiro asked.

"Not too bad," Nick told him. "You?"

Masahiro gasped for breath. "I'm okay. You've been in this situation before?" he asked Nick incredulously.

Nick nodded. "Fewer trees, and no chickens."

"Brooklyn must be hell," Masahiro said.

To Masahiro's surprise, Nick suddenly whirled and fired straight into one of the flapping white sheets on the clothesline. The sheet turned bloody and then was pulled to the ground as one of Sato's men clutched at it from behind.

Sato appeared, dragging the hysterical old woman as a shield as he made his way toward the gate. Nick and Masahiro had to hold their fire. Impotent and enraged, they watched Sato push and shove the wailing old lady through the gate. When he was safely outside, he silenced her with a single shot. Then he grabbed the bike out from under his fallen rider, grabbing up the dead man's knife and gun as well. He mounted and gunned up and headed flat-out down the road.

Thinking of nothing but Sato's getting away, Nick ran forward to grab on to the other fallen bike. He jumped on the starter and took off through the gate after Sato.

He didn't see Sato's lieutenant running toward him at full speed, leveling his weapon to fire. He had a clear target and was well within range. There was no way he could miss.

25

*I*n the same instant that Sato's guard tightened his trigger finger, Masahiro got the bead on him and got off a shot without the split-second of hesitation that would have meant Nick's life. For the first time ever, Masahiro hit the target. It was not, however, a bull's-eye—the man's thigh tore open in a red blaze, but he was still alive and his weapon was still at the ready. Masahiro fired again. To his relief, and amazement, the man fell dead in the dirt.

Nick, hearing the shots, glanced back and saw what Masahiro had done. He didn't stop to cheer. He sped through the gate and onto the dirt road, concentrating fully on the speeding figure of Sato tearing along the road winding down below, getting farther away, spitting dust in his wake as he made the curves and turns at top speed.

At full power, Nick cut diagonally overland down

the terraced hillside. He bounced a couple of feet up off the seat every time he hit a mudhole, but for the most part, the rain had soaked into the vegetable gardens and rice paddies, and the sun had started to harden the mud, just enough to prevent the terrain from killing him—barely. Astonished farmers stopped in their labors to watch as he catapulted through the air from terrace to terrace, landing with a splash and crash each time only to take off again down the hill until he gained the road.

He was close enough now to see Sato looking back over his shoulder. His wounds were bloody and obviously painful. Nick could see his whole body wince every time his bike hit a bump in the road. The back of Sato's suit jacket was glistening wet, and as Nick gained on him, he saw splotches of deep red blood that hadn't had time to dry in the tracks of Sato's wheels.

Nick was moving up on him. Sato started taking the curves with manic daring, but Nick knew this technique from his Coney Island racing days, and he followed closely into the curve, leaning the bike almost perpendicular to the ground. The road curved more radically as it wound upward; clusters of roadside trees sometimes hid one section of road from the next as they climbed. From time to time, Nick lost sight of Sato, but he kept up the speed, hoping against an ambush.

Sato was in blinding pain, and when he reached the crest of the hill, he had to stop. Gearing down his bike, he reached inside his coat and gingerly felt the wound. His hand came away covered in blood. He sat for a moment trying to catch his breath, trying to think through the pain to his next move.

Nick came to a clearing and saw the top of the rise—and Sato, sitting on his bike motionless. He rode up and stopped a few hundred yards away. They stared at each other. Neither moved; neither juiced his throttle. The earth was silent for a moment, as if their hate had formed an all-consuming vacuum.

With a shriek that pierced the silence like a razor slash, Sato screamed and twisted his throttle into action. He accelerated madly in a straight path toward Nick.

Nick saw it coming. A bellow rose from deep inside his gut as he took a gear and sped toward the onrushing Sato.

The game was "chicken" and the prize was death. They closed in at high speed.

At the last possible second, Sato veered off. Nick stayed on the deadly course, but the rear wheel of Sato's bike clipped his front wheel. Sato slid in the dirt and took a hard, excruciating spill. Nick went down, too. He had expected no less and made his body as limp and yielding as he could before he hit the hard edge of the road and rolled, dazed, into the shallow muddy water.

Through a semiconscious haze, he heard slow suction sounds, feet struggling to move against the mud. Ominous. Coming closer. He tried to sit up. Every nerve-ending was raw, but nothing seemed broken. Except maybe his head. What the hell was the thing he heard, and now saw, looming over him . . . Sato. He had managed to drag himself through the mud and now stood ankle-deep in ooze, bleeding all over his nice suit, looking down at Nick. He had the bike driver's knife in his hand. The hand was trembling but clutching the knife in a death grip.

Nick slowly pulled himself to his feet. The two men stood a few dozen yards apart, trying to muster their strength.

"We can make a deal, Conklin." Sato gasped. "You know what I have in my pocket."

They inched closer to each other.

"You hate them as much as I do," Sato said. He was obviously in pain with every breath, but he persisted. "The men in the suits . . ." he said. "Their little lives . . . petty stupid rules . . . and you deserve it. That's what you told Charlie on the plane. I heard you say it."

The two men were within striking distance of each other now. Sato raised the knife, but he was not as quick as he might have been. Nick blocked his arm.

Sato struggled and they went down together in the ankle-deep water. Their feet were glued to the thick mud, but there was something fatalistically familiar about this fight—the continuation of a match they had started in New York.

Sato was wiry, Nick had muscle. Both men were exhausted. Nick wrenched the knife out of Sato's hand and it went flying. Sato broke away, crawling on hands and knees through the mud to find the knife.

Nick struggled to his feet and stumbled after it, too, but Sato got there first. He grabbed the knife and turned back to lunge through the air at Nick, cutting him across the forehead and gashing his cheek. Nick staggered backward. Sato moved in to finish him off.

Blood ran together with the mud on Nick's face, clogging his vision and stinging like hell. He could barely see Sato coming at him, but he struck out blindly and managed to deflect the next blow. Sato's arm flew up, and through a muddy fog, Nick saw the glint of steel in the sun. He grabbed the knife from Sato and stabbed him.

Sato fell back and disappeared under the water.

When Masahiro got there, he found Nick on his knees beside Sato's body. The blood from his face mingled in the muddy water with the blood of his enemy.

"Nick?"

Nick looked up at the shadow between him and the sun that was his partner. With his last bit of energy, he showed Masahiro the slashing gesture, with his index finger, above his eyebrow, that he had learned from Sato.

Hours later, Nick and Masahiro dragged Sato into the Osaka Prefecture Headquarters. Their wounds had been attended to and Sato was bandaged like a mummy, but he was conscious. His hands were cuffed behind him. He and Nick were both still covered with mud spots, which the hospital attendants had removed from their flesh but not their clothes.

Every cop, client, criminal, cleaning person, and hanger-on in the Prefecture stopped to stare at the curious trio as they passed by on their way to the bullpen. Once in the big room, each officer turned, one by one, to watch them walk the narrow aisle between desks.

When they went into Superintendent Ohashi's office, Ohashi looked up from a report he was reading, and it was pretty clear even from his controlled reaction that he had never seen anything like this in all his years on the job. The young officer standing at his side let his jaw drop open and didn't even know it.

Nick stood off to the side. Masahiro, dried mud

clinging to his trouser legs up to the knees, stood at attention before Ohashi's desk.

"Assistant Inspector Masahiro reports the capture of the criminal fugitive Sato Koji to the superintendent," Masahiro announced in Japanese.

Ohashi stayed even. If he showed emotion his jaw would hit the desk. He cleared his throat and turned to the young officer at his side, ordered him to stop gaping and take the assistant inspector's report.

Nick stayed around for a few days, getting his wounds tended to and getting to know Masahiro's son and sharing quite a few interesting foods and one hell of a wild *sake*-drinking contest. He even tried the *karaoke* and thought he sounded pretty good for someone who couldn't carry a tune if it was in his pocket.

He spent time with Joyce, trading memories of growing up in Chicago and Brooklyn. He soaked in hot tubs and drank green tea and ate raw fish, although he drew the line at eels and octopus. He even put on a kimono a couple of times, hanging out in Joyce's place.

He bought a new suit and wore it on the day when the entire Osaka Prefecture turned out in neat ranks in the courtyard of the headquarters building. He stood with Joyce, and Masahiro's son, watching proudly as Ohashi stepped front-and-center, called out Inspector Matsumoto Masahiro, and pinned a small decoration on his breast pocket.

"Well done," Ohashi said. He saluted Masahiro. Masahiro saluted him back. Over Ohashi's shoulder, Masahiro sneaked a look at Nick, who flipped him his own version of a salute—a tiny wink.

When the ceremony was over, Joyce said, "I've got to get to work, Nick. Let's say goodbye quickly and painlessly, okay?" She smiled gloriously, her blue eyes shining.

"I never thanked you," he said.

"For what?"

"For choosing a side." He held on to her hands and kept looking into her eyes as if searching for something he wasn't sure he could find.

"Well, it turned out lucky, didn't it? And you're all over the newspapers again. A regular hero."

"Yeah . . ." Nick said. "The biggest thing to hit this town since Godzilla." He got quiet for a minute, thoughtful. "You really think you're going to last here?" he asked her.

Joyce sighed. "I don't know," she told him. "But I guess a love-hate relationship could last forever."

Nick smiled warmly. "If you ever want to see a night game at Wrigley Field I'm good for box seats," he said.

She smiled back, and walked away. Nick went to find Masahiro and his ride to the airport. Ohashi had assigned them another car and driver for the trip, only this time it was an honor.

At the airport Nick dashed into the souvenir shop while Masahiro waited for him in the *soba* restaurant. Nick bought Ninja swords for his kids and a few other things—he was feeling so good he even bought a little something for his ex. What the hell, nobody could stay mad forever. He came back to the counter and started stuffing the gifts into his duffel bag. An exceedingly loud slurp of the soft noodles from Masahiro alerted Nick that something was bothering his friend.

"I picked up some of those cotton things for anyone

I forgot," he said as he slid into the booth opposite Masahiro.

"*Yukata,*" Masahiro said. "They're less expensive in the neighborhood shops."

"Get that poor look off your face," Nick told him. Masahiro glanced up from his bowl. "I'll cover every penny you lent me," Nick said. "I put the gifts on the plastic. I was over my limit before I got here, so what the hell."

Masahiro shifted uncomfortably. "You know they never found the plates," he said gloomily. "They weren't in the farmhouse or on the road . . . they even searched a monastery near the place . . ."

Nick picked up the steaming bowl of *soba* that was waiting for him. His chopsticks guided the noodles expertly into his mouth. He slurped loudly.

"Some lucky monk is probably set for life," he said.

"I don't believe I understand," Masahiro replied.

"If a guy had both plates and knew the right people, all his problems would be solved. Who would ever know?" Nick pointed out.

Masahiro studied Nick. He put down his *soba* bowl and wondered what to believe. Nick went ahead slurping and enjoying his food.

"I think I'm getting a feel for this," he said.

The loudspeaker called Nick's plane in Japanese, English, French, and German. He grabbed his bag. "Don't come to the gate, Masa," he said, teasing. "You know how sentimental you get. It's embarrassing."

They stood up to leave the restaurant. Masahiro took a small package out of his battered little briefcase and handed it to Nick with a bow. Nick took the box, shook it, felt its heft.

"Udon?" He guessed. "Sweet plum? Pickles? I know —grilled eels—whaddya call them—"

"Kabavaki," Masahiro translated solemnly.

"You wouldn't," Nick said. "Whatever—thanks. It'll be great on the plane in case they serve any of that American shit."

He reached into his duffel. "I've got a little something here," he said. He handed Masahiro an elaborately wrapped box. It was heavy for its small size. Masahiro bowed.

"The next time you throw yourself a vacation," Nick said, "skip the cherry blossoms or the Fuji climb, and come see me instead."

Masahiro bowed again, deeply.

And Nick bowed deeply to him.

"You watch your tail, cowboy," Nick said gruffly. He turned and walked out of the restaurant without a backward glance. Masahiro watched him go, still wondering.

He looked down at the elegantly wrapped gift in his hand. He tore off the paper and took the lid off the box. Inside some tissue paper, there was an ordinary, plastic-bagged, salaryman's white shirt. He didn't want to feel disappointed, but . . . wait a minute— the box was too heavy. He lifted the shirt and looked underneath—nothing. The weight was in the baggie. He tore it open and felt through the folds of the shirt. He pulled forth both counterfeit plates. Masahiro slammed the lid on the box before anyone in the restaurant could see.

Nick was in the line filing onto the boarding ramp of the plane when Masahiro came running. "Nick!" he shouted.

They were separated by a glass wall and a crowd of

218

people, but the two men were, at that moment, closer than they had ever been. Nick waved, and then blended in with the crowd. Masahiro watched the back of Nick's head above the crush of Japanese travelers. He was the tallest man in the crowd. The biggest thing to hit this town since Godzilla.